D1095773

A Twist of Fate

THE MOSTLY MISERABLE LIFE
OF APRIL SINCLAIR

WITHDRAWN

A Twist of Fate

LAURIE FRIEDMAN

MINNEAPOLIS

Darby Creek
A division of Lerner Publishing Group, Inc.
241 First Avenue North
Minneapolis, MN 55401 USA

For reading levels and more information, look up this title
at www.lernerbooks.com.

Main body text set in Janson Text LT Std 12/17.
Typeface provided by Linotype AG.

Library of Congress Cataloging-in-Publication Data

The Cataloging-in-Publication Data for *A Twist of Fate* is on file at the Library
of Congress.
ISBN 978-1-4677-8590-7 (hardcover)
ISBN 978-1-5124-0899-7 (EB pdf)

Manufactured in the United States of America
1-37943-19401-3/7/2016

*I'd rather regret the things I've done
than the things I haven't done.*

—*Lucille Ball*

Saturday, February 28, 10:02 p.m.

I know how the saying goes—*you can't
believe everything you read.* But does that apply
to fortune-cookie fortunes?

Tonight, Mom, Dad, May, June, and I went
to Happy China for dinner, which in many
ways made me extremely happy: (a) I love
Chinese food, (b) Happy China has the best
Chinese food in Faraway, Alabama, and (c)
Dad let me order for everyone. Ever since he
opened the Love Doctor Diner, he's been the
one who orders for us when we go out. He says

he likes to pick what we get because he wants to try things that might inspire him to create new dishes at his restaurant. I say he likes to order so we get what he likes to eat.

Either way, I was surprised tonight when he said I could do it.

"We'll have the spring rolls, garlic shrimp, chicken in black bean sauce, and beef lo mein, please," I said to the server when she came to take our order.

"Excellent choices," Dad said.

When the food came, it was clear he wasn't the only one who liked my order. My family ate every bit of food on the table.

After we'd finished, the waitress brought a plate of fortune cookies. Everyone leaned in and took one. It's a Sinclair family tradition to go around the table and read our fortunes.

"Me first," said May. We all waited as she peeled the plastic wrapper from her cookie. "Romance is in your future." May frowned when she was done reading. "That's ridiculous," she said. "I don't like one boy at my school."

I poked her in the ribs. "C'mon," I said. "You're telling me there's not one boy at Faraway Middle that you like just a little bit?"

June rolled her eyes at May and me like we were both missing the point. "Read it carefully. 'In your future' could mean a long time from now, like when you're a grown-up."

"That's true," Mom said. "Also, romance doesn't only apply to relationships with other people. It could mean that you find something you have a passion for. Like a new sport."

May, June, and I all looked at Dad like we were waiting for him to give his opinion on Mom's loose definition of romance. Before he opened the Love Doctor Diner, he wrote a relationship column for the Faraway newspaper. But Dad just opened his cookie and read his fortune.

"You will enjoy travels and adventures soon to come." Dad laughed when he was done reading. "The only place I'll be going anytime soon is to the diner and back home again."

Mom read her fortune next. "Your love of the arts is one of your great gifts."

"That's true," I said, and everyone nodded.

Mom opened Flora's Fashions, a boutique of her clothing designs, in the fall. She's sold lots of clothes, not only to shoppers in Faraway but also to a big department store in Atlanta. I know she looks to the arts for inspiration.

"June, what does yours say?" asked Mom.

"Shoot for the moon. You are a star." June smiled when she was done reading. She's the top student in her grade at Faraway Elementary and an indisputable star.

"April, your turn," said Dad.

I unwrapped my cookie. "There is much rain before a rainbow." I frowned. "What kind of fortune is that?" I asked. "Is it saying I have a stormy future?"

Dad shook his head. "I take it to mean that a rainbow is on the horizon for you."

I reread my fortune. "But you can't have a rainbow before you have rain," I said.

"You can't believe everything you read in a cookie," said Mom.

Maybe Mom was right. Who knows who makes up the sayings that go in all those cookies? And really, I could have just as easily picked one cookie over another. So what's the point of getting worked up over some dumb fortune?

The answer: There is no point.

Is there?

Sunday, March 1, 9:12 p.m.

There may be more to fortunes than I thought.

Tonight, my whole family went to Gaga and Willy's house for dinner. Nothing seemed unusual. It was just Sunday night dinner with my aunts, uncles, cousins, and Sophie and her mom, Emma.

But in retrospect, there were signs something was wrong. For starters, Gaga got dinner from Lester's, which happens to serve the best barbecue in Faraway. But usually whenever Gaga invites her family to dinner, she cooks it herself.

And when we got there, dinner was already on the buffet. Gaga always waits for my mom and her sisters to help put the food out. For as long as I can remember eating at her house, the routine has been that they set everything up while the dads and kids hang out in the den, joking around and trying to guess how long Gaga has had the same mints in her candy dish.

But tonight, Gaga said she wanted to eat as soon as we'd all arrived. I guess in my head, and probably everyone else's too, dinner from Lester's was hot and ready, so we went ahead and ate it. But I definitely should have seen it as a sign. When everyone finished eating, Gaga stood up and tapped her spoon on her glass of iced tea. "May I have your attention please?"

My cousin Harry, who was sitting next to me, poked me in the ribs. I tried not to laugh. We're all used to Gaga making speeches about the meaning of life or unexpected announcements, which over the past few years have ranged from slightly entertaining to downright weird. *I'm taking up jogging. My friends and I are forming the Happiness Movement. Willy and I are getting married.* You never know what she might say.

Gaga waited until everyone was quiet. "I've always been honest and open with my family," said Gaga.

Uncle Drew gave Uncle Dusty a here-she-goes-again look. Gaga's meaning-of-life speeches can get pretty long-winded.

Gaga paused and looked at Willy, who reached over and squeezed her hand. "What I'm about to share with you isn't easy for me."

"Mom, what is it?" asked Aunt Lilly, sounding concerned.

Gaga cleared her throat and gave us all an uncharacteristically weak smile. "I have cancer."

Harry and I looked at each other, openmouthed. I have a very talkative family, but everyone sat there in complete silence, too shocked to know what to say.

Aunt Lila was the first to speak. "Are you sure?" she asked.

Gaga nodded. "I'm sure." Her voice was patient and steady, even though I was certain she thought the question was as dumb as I did. Why would she announce to her whole family that she has cancer unless she does?

Then questions erupted around the table. *What kind of cancer do you have? Which doctor have you been to? Have you gotten a second opinion? What kind of treatment is necessary? How long have you known?* Everyone was talking at once, asking Gaga questions. The room felt too loud and too warm.

Gaga tapped her spoon on her glass again and motioned for us all to settle down. "The cancer has spread throughout my body," she said.

Izzy raised her hand like we were in school. "What's cancer?" she asked.

Aunt Lila wrapped an arm around each of her six-year-old twins. "Mom, I don't think this is an appropriate conversation to be having in front of the girls."

Gaga ignored Aunt Lila and focused on Izzy. "Cancer is a sickness in your body. My cancer is in many parts of my body, which means my body is very sick."

"Do you need aspirin?" asked Charlotte.

Gaga smiled at Charlotte. "No, sweetie, I don't need an aspirin right now, but I'll let you know if I do." She looked at the rest of the family. "I know you have lots of questions," she said, like she was talking to a slew of reporters. "But this is not a complicated matter. I have cancer. At this advanced stage and at my age, surgery is not an option. I could get chemotherapy and radiation, but I'm not going to do that."

"Mom!" said Aunt Lilly. "You have to get treatment. You can't give up—"

I think the word she was going to use was *hope*. But Gaga held up her hand stop sign–style. She had more to say.

"The side effects of aggressive treatment just aren't worth the risk. Headaches. Muscle aches. Stomachaches. I'm sure there are a bunch more aches I don't even know about." Gaga paused and then continued listing symptoms. "Fatigue. Nausea. Vomiting. Diarrhea. Hair loss. Dry, itchy, blistery, peeling skin. Do you want me to keep going?"

"No," said Amanda. "We get the picture. I wouldn't want those things either."

Aunt Lilly shot her daughter a look like she shouldn't have said what she did.

I got up and got a tissue. I brought the box back with me and set it down on the table. Sophie, Emma, and Mom took one. Everyone looked upset. The idea that Gaga was so sick was awful, but what she was describing didn't sound good either. It was like someone had given her two bad choices and told her to pick one.

"I hope you all understand that I don't want to lie around, sick and uncomfortable, in a hospital bed with a bunch of needles stuck in me," said Gaga.

"Mom!" said Aunt Lila. "The kids don't need to hear any more."

But that didn't stop Gaga. "I'm eighty years old. I want to spend the little time I have left doing things I've always wanted to do. Haven't you ever heard of a bucket list?"

"I have," said June.

"Me too," said May.

Gaga smiled at my younger sisters. "Good," she said. "Then you'll understand what I'm about to say. Going skiing with my family is at the top of my bucket list. I've always wanted to learn to ski, and it's high time I got around to it."

She paused. "Willy and I have rented a large condo in Park City, Utah, for the week of spring break. We want all of you to come skiing with us. There's plenty of room, and we'll take care of everything—transportation, gear, ski school. All the arrangements will be made. All you have to do is say yes."

I saw my uncles smile at each other. Cancer or not, Gaga was still being Gaga, and I think they were both relieved to see it.

"Mom, do you really think this is a good idea?" asked Aunt Lilly.

"I think it's a great idea," said Gaga.

"What about the altitude? Is it even safe to travel in your condition?"

"A change of scenery does a body good," said Gaga. It wasn't an answer to Aunt Lilly's questions, but it was a very Gaga thing to say. She put a hand on Willy's shoulder. He stood up, wrapped an arm around Gaga, and gave her a quick peck on the cheek. Harry and I always joke that their public displays of affection are kind of nauseating, but neither of us said a word.

Gaga cleared her throat. "Willy and I are going skiing with or without you," she said. I honestly thought she was going to ask for a show of hands to see who was in, but she didn't. All she said was that she understood it was a lot to take in and that we should get back to her and let her know if we're planning to go.

Then she picked up a stack of plates and carried them into the kitchen. It was her way of saying we were dismissed.

When we got in the car to go home, everyone was very quiet.

June finally broke the silence. "Dad's fortune last night at the restaurant said he would travel soon. It's coming true," she said.

"No one has made any decisions about the trip yet," Mom said.

"Is Gaga going to die?" asked May.

"Everyone dies," said June.

Mom got teary-eyed. Dad reached over and squeezed her shoulder. "Flora, it's going to be OK," he said.

Dad is usually pretty good about saying stuff that makes a person feel better, but I thought what he'd said was lame. How was that supposed to make Mom feel better?

Gaga is the backbone of our family. She's what holds it all up. As we drove the short distance home, I kept asking myself one question.

When something happens to Gaga, how's it going to be OK?

10:02 p.m.
Sophie called

Sophie just called, and I got the after-report. "After you all left, it was bad," she said. "Gaga started crying."

Since Sophie's parents split at the end of the summer, Sophie and her mom moved to Faraway to live with Sophie's grandpa, Willy, and Gaga. That makes Sophie my best source for inside information.

"Do you think she was crying because she doesn't feel well?" I asked.

"Do you mean physically well?" asked Sophie.

"I guess." I wasn't really sure what I meant.

"I think it upset her to tell her family," said Sophie. "And it upset my grandpa to see her upset. I heard him tell my mom he's not ready to lose her."

I don't blame him. They've only been married a little over a year. "It's unfair," I said to Sophie.

"It is," she said. Then she paused like she was thinking. "Maybe it's fate. You know, maybe they met later in life so they'd have someone to spend their last few years with."

"Yeah," I said. "Maybe." But as I hung up the phone, I wasn't so sure.

I've always thought of fate in a fairy-tale sort of way. The beautiful princess meets the handsome prince. They fight off an evil witch or a pack of bad guys and live happily ever after.

I guess when you get married at eighty, you know your happily ever after is limited. Still, that's pretty different from knowing it's right around the corner.

10:54 p.m.
Just called Leo

After I talked to Sophie, part of me didn't want any other friends to know about Gaga being sick. I felt like it would make it more real if other people knew. But a bigger part of me needed to talk about it, so I called Leo.

He's still my go-to person, even though he's off in college, at age sixteen. Especially lately, since Brynn and I aren't friends anymore, and Billy and Sophie started going out. I figured Leo would know what to say. No matter what the topic, he always has some insightful bit to add. But when I finished telling him what I found out at dinner, Leo was uncharacteristically quiet.

"That sucks," he finally said.

What else is there to say?

Nothing is creepier than a bunch of adults being very quiet.

—Tina Fey

Monday, March 2, 9:17 p.m.
In my room, thinking about what I heard
And what I didn't

When I got home from dance practice, Aunt Lilly, Aunt Lila, and my mom were at the kitchen table. Mom had her laptop open, and there were papers, pens, and coffee cups everywhere. I imagine it's what a presidential campaign strategy session might look like, but given what Gaga told us last night, I was pretty sure Mom and her sisters weren't discussing politics.

"April, there's pizza," Mom said, motioning to the box on the counter. "Take a slice and you can eat dinner in the family room with May and June."

I knew that meant she wanted me to take my pizza and go because they were discussing something she didn't want me to hear. But in my opinion, a kitchen in a house full of people is no place to carry on a private conversation. Plus, I was curious about what they were saying.

I put a slice of mushroom pizza on a plate and then filled a mug with water and put it in the microwave. As the sound from the microwave filled the room, everyone at the table looked at me like they wanted an explanation as to why I was still there.

"I'm making tea," I said.

"Tea with pizza?" Aunt Lilly asked, like that was an unheard-of combination.

"I like tea with pizza." I turned around to face the microwave. As I watched the clock counting down the time, I hoped they'd forget I was there and keep talking. It seemed to work.

"We have to intervene," said Aunt Lilly. "We'll just tell Mom we're taking her to the medical center in Birmingham for a second opinion. I already have a list of doctors we can call." I heard the shuffling of papers.

"She's a grown woman," my mom reminded her older sister. "You can't just make her do something she's already told you she doesn't want to do."

When the microwave beeped, my mom and aunts all looked at me. "Is your tea ready?" Mom asked.

"Almost," I said as I slowly took the teabag out of the box and got the milk from the refrigerator and the honey out of the pantry. Mom gave me a hurry-up look but then went back to the conversation with her sisters.

"She trusts Dr. Green, and she knows how she wants to handle this," said Mom in a low voice. "I think we need to respect that."

"Well, I disagree with how she's handling it," said Aunt Lilly. Her voice was anything but low. It was obvious she was agitated that Mom wasn't in agreement with her.

"What about the trip?" asked Aunt Lila. "We haven't even discussed it. Mom really wants us to all go."

"If we all stick together on this and say we're not going, it will force her to cancel the trip," said Aunt Lilly.

"Like a boycott?" I asked. I hadn't meant to interject, but it just slipped out.

My mom and aunts all looked at me. "April, take your tea and pizza into the other room," Mom said.

Stalling was no longer an option, so I went into the family room and watched *SpongeBob* with my sisters while I ate. When we finished, the conversation in the kitchen was still going strong.

I took the dinner plates into the kitchen and started to wash them in the sink. As a card-carrying member of this family, I felt I had the right to know what was being said, but apparently Mom disagreed. "April, leave the plates on the counter, please, and go do your homework, and make sure May and June do theirs too." Her voice was all business.

I started my homework, but I had a hard time focusing on the biological behavior of plants when I was a whole lot more interested in the behavior that was going on in the kitchen between my mother and her sisters. Their voices were elevated, which meant they weren't in agreement on what was being discussed. I couldn't make out what they were saying, but from what I'd heard earlier, Aunt Lilly wants to get a second opinion and definitely not go on the trip. Mom wants to respect what Gaga wants, and if I had to guess, Aunt Lila hasn't made her mind up about how she feels. It sounds like she's more Team Mom than Team Aunt Lilly, but I'm not sure.

When I heard the front door shut a few minutes ago, I looked at my watch. My aunts were already at my house when I got home at 5:45, and they left at 9:02. That means they talked for at least three hours and seventeen minutes, maybe longer.

So I know how long they were talking . . . but what I really want to know is what was said.

Today I found out what was going on last
night between my mom and my aunts, but now
I have something new to wonder about.

I ate lunch with Harry and Sophie, and
Harry told us that his mom was really upset
when she got home last night. He said he
heard her telling his dad that she thinks
my mom and Aunt Lila are ganging up on
her. She said that they all agreed to be on
the same page, but she thinks it's crazy to
let Gaga go on a trip when she's sick, and
my mom and Aunt Lila think we should all
respect Gaga's wishes.

"I didn't know grown-ups could gang up on
one another," I said.

"Anyone can gang up," said Harry. "But I'm
glad they did. Amanda and I agree with Aunt
Flora and Aunt Lila. Not just because we want
to go skiing. We think Gaga should get to
choose what she wants to do. It's not like she's
a child."

"I totally agree," I said between bites of my

21

tuna wrap. Harry and I both looked at Sophie for her to weigh in. I was sure she was going to agree with us. She's usually the poster child for letting people have free choice.

"Huh?" Sophie looked like she hadn't been paying any attention to what we were talking about. I repeated the details of the debate between the sisters. But when I finished, Sophie had this weird, blank look like she hadn't heard a word I'd said.

I waved my hands in front of her face. "Earth to Sophie."

"Oh, sorry," she said like she just realized her lack of interest was obvious. Then she muttered something about having a test and left.

"That was weird," I said.

"Yeah," said Harry. "A lot of weird things are going on in our family lately."

I had to agree. Gaga is sick. Mom and her sisters are fighting, and Sophie is suddenly all loopy and distracted. I don't usually think of Harry as a particularly good barometer of human emotion, but today I'd say he was spot on.

Wednesday, March 4, 5:58 p.m.

When I got home from dance, there was a note from Mom saying that she was at Aunt Lila's, Dad was at the diner, and there was meatloaf and green beans for May, June, and me in the oven.

Translation: Mom and her sisters are back at it.

10:42 p.m.

Leo just called, which was good because it made me stop listening to the conversation that was going on across the hall in Mom and Dad's room, about the fact that Aunt Lilly is now officially not talking to Mom or Aunt Lila. Listening to Mom tell Dad what was going on was making me feel sick. It's bad enough that Gaga has cancer, but it just seems like completely the wrong time for my mom and her sisters to be fighting, when they have always been close.

"April, you're kind of quiet," Leo said a few minutes into our conversation. "I find it odd you have no comment on the fact that the highly esteemed university I go to is no longer offering ham or turkey as fillings at the make-your-own omelet station."

I couldn't help but giggle. Leo knows me well enough to know I would normally have a lot to say on a topic like that. "Sorry," I said. "I guess my mind was elsewhere."

"Care to share?" asked Leo.

I'd already told him about Gaga's cancer, but this latest dramatic development was new news.

"Hmmm," said Leo when I was done talking. I gave him time to think.

"There's a political principle called *majority rule*," he said when he finally spoke. "It's a system that gives the majority, usually constituted by fifty-one percent of an organized group, the power to make decisions binding upon the whole."

"You sound like a dictionary," I said.

"Thanks," said Leo, like there was no higher compliment. "It might help matters if your mom and Aunt Lila acquaint your Aunt Lilly with this principle."

"You're a genius," I said to Leo.

"Not really," said Leo. "A genius wouldn't have told you about this principle, because if it works, it means you'll be off skiing in Utah when I return to Faraway for spring break."

He had a point there. But honestly, Aunt Lilly can be pretty stubborn, and it's going to take a lot more than some fancy principle to get her to change her mind.

Friday, March 6, 8:15 p.m.
It's official

My family is all in. We're going to Park City, Utah, to go skiing.

But it was NOT an easy decision. There was a lot of debate all week about what to do. Aunt Lilly wanted everyone to say they wouldn't go on the trip, in hopes that Gaga would cancel it and stay home and see more doctors.

Aunt Lilly finally gave in and went along with Mom and Aunt Lila, who both felt Gaga should get to decide what she wants to do. But it wasn't Leo's majority rule principle that swayed her. Harry and Amanda did the trick.

They both told Aunt Lilly they feel strongly that at age eighty, Gaga should get to make her own decisions.

Gaga is thrilled that we're all going, but now she's stressed. She's knitting ski caps for all of us. That's seventeen caps in two weeks, which Gaga says is a lot, even for a super-knitter like herself. I've seen the wool she's using, and it's neon orange. When I told her it's kind of bright, she said it'll make us easy to spot in a snowstorm. No doubt she's right.

Aunt Lilly tried to convince Gaga not to knit the caps. She said it would exhaust her. But Gaga said that knitting matching ski caps for her family is the second item on her bucket list, and then she laughed like she thought that was hysterically funny.

So in two weeks, my whole weird, opinionated, soon-to-be-neon-orange-capped family is going to Utah to go skiing.

Park City, get ready.

The true mystery of the world is the visible, not the invisible.

—*Oscar Wilde*

Sunday, March 8, 4:45 p.m.
What's up with Sophie?

Whatever's going on with Sophie is a big mystery. I know she doesn't have chicken pox, the flu, or scarlet fever. But something's up, and I have no idea what it is.

This afternoon, Sophie and I were trying to do some online shopping for ski clothes. But I was the only one shopping. Sophie was off in la-la land. I had to ask her at least six times to pay attention, but even that didn't work.

Finally I said, "Sophie, I'm counting on you

to make good choices." I pointed to the two of us. "You and me. We're both heading to Utah in less than two weeks, and you're the head shopper here. Help me, help us!" I tried to say it in a funny way. She knows I trust her taste in clothes more than I trust my own. I thought it would make her laugh and focus, but it didn't.

She just sat there staring at the screen, even though she wasn't paying any attention to what was on it. I kept showing her different ski pants and jackets, and no matter what I showed her, she said it was cute. Finally as a test, I showed her a picture of a frog and said, "Do you like these ski pants?"

"Cute," she said.

I closed my laptop. "You just said a frog is cute. Is there something you're not telling me?" I asked.

Sophie gave me this weird, blank look. I have no clue what it meant. Then she reached over and opened my laptop. "Let's just shop, OK?"

"Sure," I said. But it was pretty obvious her heart wasn't in it.

8:02 p.m.
Talked to Mom

All night I've been thinking about Sophie and how spaced out she was this afternoon. And it wasn't the first time it happened. I thought back to the other day at lunch when Harry and I were talking about whether we should go on the trip, and Sophie didn't even have an opinion. It's so not like Sophie. She's usually chatty and upbeat, and she always has a pithy (vocab word) comment to make about whatever subject we're talking about.

So tonight as I was helping Mom wash the dishes after dinner, I decided to see if she had any insight into what's going on. "Hey, Mom," I said as I dried a casserole dish, "Has Emma talked to you lately about Sophie?"

My mom and Emma have gotten closer since Sophie and Emma moved in with Gaga and Willy. So I figured if something was up with Sophie, Emma would tell Mom.

But Mom just shook her head. "Emma hasn't mentioned a thing. Did Sophie do something unusual?"

I told Mom how Sophie was zoned out when we were ordering things online this afternoon and about what happened at lunch with Harry.

"Hmm," said Mom when I finished. "I wouldn't read much into two isolated incidents."

I dried my hands on a dishtowel. "You're probably right," I said.

But . . . what if she isn't?

10:22 p.m.
Talked to Leo

When Leo called, I told him what's been going on with Sophie. "Mom doesn't think it's anything," I said. "But I'm not so sure." I asked if he thought it sounded like two isolated incidents.

"As opposed to what? A pattern?" asked Leo.

I hadn't really thought about it like that. "I guess," I said.

"In that case, I agree with your mom. Two incidents, albeit ones that are indicative of a brain being elsewhere, don't form a consistent pattern."

"How many incidents does it take to make a pattern?" I asked.

"Good question," said Leo. "Unfortunately, I don't have an answer.

"That's the best you can do?" I asked.

Leo paused for a minute, like he was thinking. "I think you'll know a pattern when you see one."

"What if I don't want to see a pattern? What I want is for Sophie to snap out of whatever funk she's in and start acting like herself again."

"In that case," said Leo, "why not hope for the best?"

"Sure," I said. But it begs the question: Do I need to prepare for the worst?

Wednesday, March 11
Talked to Billy

Billy just called me with his own weird story about Sophie. "Student Government is doing a skit at the assembly the Friday before spring break," he said. "Today, we were in the middle of rehearsal, and Sophie left."

"Where'd she go?" I asked.

"To take a phone call."

I had to laugh. Billy made it sound like Sophie was an important business executive, and the image of her in a suit and heels was kind of silly.

"It wasn't funny," said Billy. "Sophie has the lead role in the skit. There are nine other people in the skit who couldn't continue rehearsing without her," he said. When he told me she was gone for fifteen minutes, I realized it really wasn't funny. Student Government is so important to Sophie, and I know she wouldn't just walk out of a rehearsal and make everyone else wait for her.

"Who do you think she was talking to?" I asked Billy.

"I don't know," he said. "When we were done, I asked her, and she wouldn't tell me. So I asked if something was wrong."

"What'd she say?"

"She said she didn't want to talk about it," said Billy.

"What do you think that means?" I asked.

Billy let out a breath into the phone. "That means something's wrong."

Leo had said I'll know a pattern when I see one. I think I see one.

Friday the 13th, 6:15 p.m.
At home

The ski clothes we ordered online arrived today, and for sure, someone put a hex on the items in the box. "You look like a stuffed panda," June said when I tried on the puffy jacket and pants. Sophie had obviously been off her game when we shopped online.

"Maybe it will look better if you roll up the pants," said May.

I shook my head.

"What if you tuck the jacket into the pants?" she asked.

"No one tucks their jacket into their pants." I know May was trying to be helpful, but I didn't think I should have to tell her that.

When Mom saw me, she bit her lip like she was trying not to laugh. The sad truth was that no amount of rolling or tucking was going to make my ski pants look any better.

And apparently, I'm not the only member of my family who had online shopping troubles. Everyone ordered stuff, and no one was satisfied with everything they got.

So tomorrow, my whole family is taking a road trip to Mobile to go shopping for ski clothes. It was Gaga's idea. She says she never thought the online shopping thing was going to work and that she has everything "under control." When I asked Gaga what she meant by that, she said I'd have to wait and see.

I'm waiting. But something tells me I'm not going to like what I see.

I am still determined to be cheerful
and to be happy in whatever
situation I may be.

—*Martha Washington*

Saturday, March, 14, 5:59 p.m.
Back from Mobile

NEWSFLASH: My parents allowed me to ride in a car driven by Harry from Faraway to Mobile. He's seventeen, so in my opinion, that makes him perfectly qualified to drive the fifty-five minutes it takes to get from Faraway to Mobile. But he doesn't have a lot of experience on the highway, so when he said he was driving Amanda and asked if Sophie and I could go with them, I was pretty shocked when Emma and my mom both said yes.

Emma is normally really protective of Sophie. So when Sophie said she wanted to ride with Harry, I thought for sure Emma was going to say something about how Harry is an inexperienced driver or that it would be nice if she and Sophie rode together with Gaga and Willy. But Emma just said OK, almost as if it was a battle she was choosing not to fight.

It didn't leave Mom with much of a choice when Harry asked if it was OK if I rode with them too. "Sure," she said. But I was pretty sure she only said it because she didn't want to make it seem like she was the only one who didn't trust Harry.

As Amanda, Sophie, Harry, and I drove from Faraway to Mobile, we talked about all sorts of things.

We tried to guess what the surprise would be that Gaga promised she had waiting for all of us when we get to the store. We placed bets on how many days during the trip my mom, Aunt Lilly, and Aunt Lila would wear matching ski sweaters. And we joked around about how funny our parents would look in their long underwear. When Harry started describing what each of the grown-ups would look like, Amanda and I were cracking up, but Sophie was quiet. She was busy texting.

"Are you texting your boyfriend?" Amanda asked Sophie. When Sophie didn't respond, Amanda reached over and plucked Sophie's phone from her hand. "Ooh! Whatever you're writing must be juicy!" she said.

Amanda probably shouldn't have taken Sophie's phone, but it was clear from her tone that she was just messing around. Unfortunately, Sophie didn't see it that way.

She snatched her phone from Amanda and shoved it into her pocket. "It's none of your business who I'm texting!" Her voice had a sharp edge to it. She turned toward the window like she'd rather look at the fields of cows we were passing than anyone else in the car. A long silence settled over the four of us.

Amanda finally broke it. "I'm sorry," she said.

"No big deal," Sophie mumbled. But she just continued to stare out the window. Clearly, whoever she was texting with and whatever she was texting about was a bigger deal than she was letting on.

As we pulled into the parking lot of the ski store, I thought about trying to talk to Sophie, but it would have been hard to have a heart-to-heart then and there. Plus, as soon as we walked into the store, Gaga said it was time for our surprise. "Larry, we're here!" she shouted as we walked inside.

Larry, the manager, magically materialized. "I've been waiting for you," he said.

I believed him. He looked lottery-winner happy to see us as he led all seventeen of us to the back of the store, and I soon found out why.

"Here they are!" he said to Gaga. He opened a large box and started pulling out pair after pair of bright green ski pants. When he was done, he opened another box that held matching jackets.

"Larry is having a special on these," Gaga said as she slipped on a jacket. "He was waiting for us to arrive before he put them out."

"It wouldn't have mattered," Harry mumbled. "No one would have touched them." I clamped my lips together. I didn't want to say anything rude and hurt Gaga's feelings, but I couldn't have agreed more.

"What if someone wants a different color?" asked Amanda.

Everyone looked at Gaga. Aunt Lilly shot Amanda a look. "The color is fabulous," said Aunt Lilly. Then she looked around at all of the kids. "No one would want a different color." It was clearly more of an order than a statement.

Gaga seemed unfazed. "Larry has these in every size so we should all be able to find the right fit," she said. As he passed out ski pants and jackets for everyone to try on, she was the only person smiling bigger than he was.

When I looked in the mirror at my jacket and pants, I tried to focus on the positives. The pants and jacket weren't oversized and puffy, like the ones I'd ordered online. On the flip side, they were just so glaringly green. And I know I wasn't the only one who thought so. As Uncle Drew and Uncle Dusty emerged from their dressing rooms, the looks on their faces said it all. But no one said anything.

Except for May. "Do these come in red?" she asked Larry.

Everyone turned to look at her. I couldn't believe she'd asked the question. She's the least fashion conscious person I know. Plus, it was pretty clear that Aunt Lilly wasn't just talking to Amanda when she gave the warning that no one should say anything about the color.

"Seafoam green is the only color that looks universally good on any skin type," said Mom, like she was giving a fashion designer's point of view on things. I knew what she was really doing was diverting the attention away from May. The outfits were clearly more neon than seafoam, but no one contradicted Mom.

"They'll coordinate perfectly with the hats I'm knitting," Gaga said happily.

I couldn't help but think that the only place those two colors coordinate is side by side in a box of Day-Glo markers.

"My second favorite color is all shades of

green," said Izzy. "I love my ski suit."

"Me too," said Charlotte.

"I knew you'd all be pleased!" Gaga said. I wasn't sure if she was oblivious to what was going on or just happy that we all had what we needed to go skiing. "Larry, ring us up." She clapped her hands together like it was time to complete the purchase.

"I'm speechless," Amanda whispered to Harry and me when none of the grown-ups were in earshot.

"Let's look on the bright side," said Harry. "Scratch that—let's hope no one looks on the bright side, because we're it."

It was pretty hard to watch as Larry bagged up our purchases. I don't want to sound ungrateful, particularly given the reason we're going on the trip. But seventeen people ranging in age from six to eighty hitting the slopes in neon-green ski suits, not to mention the traffic-stopping orange hats Gaga is knitting, is just weird.

I'm sure weirder things have happened. But I can't imagine what.

Tuesday, March 17, 7:45 p.m.
Training camp vs. skiing
No-brainer

Something's going on with May. It's like all
of a sudden, she's become the most thoughtless
version of herself. I hope it's just a phase. If not,
it's a problem.

Tonight, Dad was working late at the diner,
so Mom, May, June, and I were eating chicken
and rice that Mom made when May brought
up the spring-break training camp her softball
coach planned for the team.

"Coach Greer said it's important for the
team to have that time to train together. I need
to be here for it," said May.

I was shocked she brought it up to Mom,
especially so close to the trip. May plays for the
Faraway Middle School softball team. It's not
exactly Major League Baseball. I get that she
wants to be part of an important team activity, but
she knows the reason we're going on the trip.

Plus, it wasn't the first rude remark she'd
made lately. When she asked at the store if the
ski suits came in red, Mom came to her rescue.

Usually she's surprisingly sensitive. I wanted to shake May and say, *"Who are you, and what have you done with my sister?"* I also wanted to defend Mom, which isn't typical.

I looked at my middle sister. "Don't you think you're being pretty insensitive? What are you going to do while the rest of us go skiing?"

"I could stay home and dog-sit Gilligan," she said.

I had to laugh. May has never so much as toasted a piece of bread. I think Gilligan is more qualified to be in charge than she is. Plus, she knows Gilligan is staying with our next-door neighbors, the Coopers, while we're gone.

"What would you eat? How would you get around?" asked Mom.

May scratched her head like she was actually composing her answers.

"I don't think you're supposed to answer those questions," said June. "They were rhetorical."

I smiled. At least one of my sisters got it.

"I'm sorry you have to miss training camp," said Mom. "But you know you can't stay home."

"Then I have to write Coach Greer a note about why I can't attend. What should I say?" asked May.

Before Mom had a chance to answer, June jumped in again. "Why don't you say you have to go skiing with our grandmother because she's going to die?" She paused for a minute like she was thinking. "Or you could just write that we're going skiing and leave out the part about Gaga dying."

June is so smart. I love that she knows what a rhetorical question is and that she always has her own thoughts about things, no matter the topic. But I felt a little heartsick when she answered May's question about the note to Coach Greer. I wish there were a way we could leave out the part about Gaga dying.

And not just in the note.

Wednesday, March 18, 6:45 p.m.
Talked to Sophie

Sophie has been quiet and withdrawn all week. I've tried several times to talk to her, but every time we've been alone, she's scampered off like she had somewhere else to be. It's clear she's trying to avoid me, but I have no idea why.

It makes me wonder if I did something to upset her. Today I was determined to find out. When I saw her go into the bathroom after lunch, I followed her in. I positioned myself right in front of her stall, which made me pretty hard to avoid. "What's going on with you?" I asked as she came out.

"Huh?" she said as she ducked around me.

I followed her to the sink. "I know something's wrong. I'm your best friend." I waited when she dried her hands on a paper towel.

"I'm fine," she said as she started to walk out of the bathroom.

I could have let it go, but I didn't. I followed after her. Even though I was frustrated that she wouldn't tell me what's going on, I didn't want it to seem that way. "Sophie, you can tell me anything," I said. I made a conscious effort to make my voice sound as sweet and soft as possible. I wanted her to know I would always be there for her.

She didn't respond, so I tried again. "Lately, it just seems like you've been upset."

She shrugged like she didn't care how it seemed.

She wasn't making it easy. I took a deep breath. "I talked to Billy last night. He said he tried to talk to you, and you wouldn't tell him what's wrong either. Did I do something to upset you? Did Billy?"

Sophie stopped walking and looked at me. "I'm going through some stuff. It'll work out. I know you're trying to be a good friend, but I don't want to talk about it. OK?"

"OK," I said. What else was there to say? I just hope whatever *it* is, it works out before we go on the ski trip.

Friday, March 20, 9:45 p.m.
Last day of school

Today was the last day of school before spring break, which is always a great day. Teachers know students aren't in work mode, and I don't think they are either, actually. Ms. Monteleone brought doughnuts to homeroom. Mr. Baumgartner gave us a study period in algebra, and we watched a movie in English.

My day was easy and almost completely great, with the exception of the two minutes I spent stuck in the bathroom, waiting in line behind Brynn for a stall.

It's hard to believe we were best friends since kindergarten, and now we don't even speak to each other, but that's the way it is. We've barely spoken since we fought on New Year's Day. Even though we have dance-team practice together every afternoon, we've worked out an elaborate system to avoid each other. But today when I ended up in line in the bathroom behind her, it would have been too weird not to say something.

"Do you have plans for spring break?" I asked.

"I'm going to Greece with my parents," she said.

It was my turn. "Wow. That's cool. I'm sure you'll have fun."

"Yeah," said Brynn.

I waited for her to ask what I'm doing for spring break, but she didn't. I thought about telling her about Gaga. Brynn always loved her. When we were little, we used to go to Gaga's house and make collages out of her sewing scraps. Part of me thought she might want to know that Gaga is sick. But most of me thought she wouldn't. For all I know, she already knows. I'm sure my mom told her mom. But who knows if her mom told her.

When a stall became available, she went in without saying another word to me.

As I waited, I couldn't help but think it was ironic. We used to talk all the time. Once in sixth grade, we spent over two hours discussing what kind of jeans we were going to wear to Kelly Blake's birthday party. When we finally decided that she was going with black skinny jeans and I was going to wear white ripped jeans, as opposed to me wearing black skinny jeans and her wearing white ripped ones, we couldn't believe how long we'd talked about one subject, and such a trivial one. We actually made a joke about setting a world record for it.

Things have definitely changed.

We don't talk to each other anymore—not about friends or boys or camp or clothes. We don't talk about anything.

Including sick grandmothers.

9:34 p.m.
Packed
Going to sleep

At this time tomorrow, I will be going to sleep seven thousand feet above sea level. That's the altitude of Park City, Utah. It's quite possible that when I get there, I will experience altitude sickness.

I didn't even know there was such a thing, but tonight at dinner, Dad told us that when you're not used to higher altitudes, you can experience symptoms that include headache, fatigue, stomach illness, dizziness, and trouble sleeping.

I've got a sick grandmother, a best friend who is clearly consumed with some personal issue she doesn't want to share with me, a younger sister who is going through a selfish phase or possibly is just becoming selfish, and now altitude sickness to worry about.

Ready or not, mountain ski trip, here I come.

I can't promise I'll try,

but I'll try to try.

—Bart Simpson

Saturday, March 21, 5:30 a.m.
DAY 1
On the plane

It's only 5:30 in the morning, and I'm already seated on a plane. I'm dressed and fed. I've driven the hour it takes to get from Faraway to the airport in Mobile, then checked my bag, gone through security, and boarded the plane, where I'm now sitting in a middle seat between my two younger sisters. In my opinion, one might wonder why the oldest of three siblings didn't get the aisle or a window seat.

Here's the unfortunate answer: The grown-ups who booked these first-thing-in-the-morning flights didn't think through the consequences of waking up young humans at 3:45 a.m. to make these flights. May and June have been cranky and fighting since we got up this morning. So now, I'm stuck in a middle seat because Mom put me here to separate them.

Wheels up in thirty. Not quite the start I'd hoped for.

10:00 a.m.
Atlanta airport, food court

We're almost two hours into our three-hour layover in the Atlanta airport, and I'm amazed at what I've learned since we've been here.

One: In addition to coffee, bagels, biscuits, eggs, and pretty much any other food that has ever been classified as a breakfast offering, at the Atlanta airport, you can also purchase a sandwich, pizza, barbecue, Chinese food, frozen yogurt, and fried chicken all before ten in the morning. Also, the calorie content of many of these foods is not only high but also readily available. I know this because June looked at every food vendor we've passed to see if they post how many calories are in their menu options, and then she'd make an announcement about the most calorie-rich food on the menu.

Two: Charlotte and Izzy had the stomach flu all week, and they almost didn't come on the trip. No one was supposed to know they'd been sick. But everyone found out when we got to the food court, because Charlotte asked Aunt Lila if she and Izzy could have fried chicken for breakfast or if it would hurt their stomachs.

Then she announced to the group that she wanted to know because she and Izzy had been sick, and the only things they'd been allowed to eat were rice, apples, crackers, and bananas.

When she started to describe their

symptoms, which were pretty disgusting to listen to, Izzy reminded Charlotte that they weren't supposed to tell anyone they'd been sick. Everyone looked at Aunt Lila, who clearly had been the one to instruct them to keep that information secret. She said the girls have been well since Thursday and aren't contagious. Honestly, I'm not so sure. They both look a little pale and sickly to me.

Three: Amanda's boyfriend of three weeks broke up with her. I learned this when we got to the food court, and Aunt Lilly asked Amanda what she was going to eat, and Amanda said nothing. When Aunt Lilly said she had to eat something, Amanda reminded her that she's on a partial hunger strike. It is apparently making her very irritable, because when she found out Charlotte and Izzy had been sick, she told them both that if she spends the week puking, she'd going to take them to the top of the tallest, snowiest mountain and leave them on it.

When she said that, Gaga hugged Charlotte and Izzy and said, "Over my dead body!" Pretty much everyone except for Gaga looked horrified when she said it. Gaga actually laughed like she appreciated the irony of her statement.

Aunt Lilly clearly didn't. She took Amanda by the arm and led her away from the group. She gave her what Gaga calls "a good old-fashioned talking to." And she didn't do it quietly. I heard every word Aunt Lilly said (as did many other people in the Atlanta airport, including Gaga). She told Amanda that she shouldn't have to remind her that we should all be on our best behavior around Gaga and only say positive things to her so we don't upset her. I know she wants the trip to be as easy and pleasant as possible for Gaga. I respect that, but I personally don't think talks like the one Aunt Lilly gave Amanda make the trip all that pleasant. Not that anyone asked Gaga, but if they did, I'm sure she would have agreed.

Four: Harry thinks Gaga should be allowed to say whatever she wants to say. Even things like, "Over my dead body!"

When Aunt Lilly finished her talk with Amanda, Harry told his mother that *over my dead body* is just an expression and that she shouldn't get bent out of shape about the fact that Gaga said it.

That prompted Gaga to weigh in. "Just because I have cancer doesn't mean you can't be honest with me," Gaga said. She said it to the whole group but looked at Aunt Lilly as she spoke.

"Mom, you're the one who started the Happiness Movement. You're the one who always talks about how important it is to be positive," said Aunt Lilly.

"That's true," said Gaga. "I do believe in happiness and positivity, but it's important to be realistic and accept what you can't change."

I'm not sure if that counts as one of the things I've learned in the airport. I think I probably already knew it. But Aunt Lilly and Gaga continued talking about it for the rest of the layover, so at the very least, I can say that it was clearly reinforced.

Five: Emma and Sophie aren't getting along

as well as they usually do, and I'm beginning to wonder if it has something to do with why Sophie has been in a funk.

They had what seemed like a really stupid argument over Starbucks. Emma, who had gotten in line, got Sophie a vanilla Frappuccino. When she gave it to her, Sophie said it wasn't what she ordered.

"I asked for an Americano with steamed soy," Sophie said to Emma. Honestly, Sophie sounded uncharacteristically bratty when she said it. Then, when Emma apologized for getting the wrong drink and said that Sophie always gets a vanilla Frappuccino, Sophie said, "Oh my God. You don't ever listen to what I want."

It was pretty clear they weren't just discussing coffee.

Six: My horoscope for the week is bad. June, who has been into reading horoscopes lately, told me that mine said the upcoming week is a bad time for me to travel. It kind of freaked me out, since traveling is exactly what I'm doing this week. Plus, I couldn't help but think about the fortune cookies we got. Dad's fortune about traveling came true. Mine said rain was coming my way, and the next day I found out my grandmother is dying of cancer. I said a quick prayer for horoscopes to be a lot less accurate than fortune-cookie fortunes.

Seven: Last but not least, I learned that the ski conditions in Park City are excellent. The mountains are covered in fresh snow. While we're there, it's going to be clear and sunny, with temperatures in the low thirties during the days, dropping into the twenties at night. Uncle Drew was the one who gave us that weather forecast. He isn't a big talker, but he loves following the weather and always makes it his mission to make sure anyone who goes anywhere with him is fully aware of atmospheric conditions.

When Uncle Drew gave us the weather report, I told Gaga how excited I am to get to Park City and see the snow-covered mountains. As soon as I said it, I felt kind of bad. I wanted her to know I was excited,

but not for the reason behind the trip.
"What I meant to say is that I'm excited to
go on the trip but that I wish it were under
different conditions."

Gaga laughed. "The ski conditions are
excellent. What more could you want?"

I frowned. Gaga knew I meant her
condition. She wrapped her arm around me.
"No need to be a drama queen. Just enjoy the
trip. Deal?"

"Deal," I said.

Aunt Lilly just told us all to pack it
up. It's time to go to our gate. To be
continued . . . mountainside.

9:02 p.m., Park City time
(11:02 p.m., Faraway time)
In bed

It has been a very long day, starting at 3:45
a.m. Faraway time, which is 1:45 a.m. Park
City time, which means I've been awake for . . .
way too long. If I weren't so tired, I'd do the
math to figure out just how long that is. At
least we're here.

We landed in Salt Lake City this afternoon, and of the twenty-four bags we checked, only one was lost, and it belonged to Amanda. She was going on and on in the airport about how bad things always happen to her—boyfriends break up with her, airlines lose her luggage. Gaga reminded Amanda there are worse things, which shut Amanda up. The good news is that the airline found her bag and delivered it to our condo tonight.

After we got our bags, we rented two giant vans and drove to our condo in Park City. As we drove through the mountains on the way to Park City, I couldn't believe how huge and beautiful they were. It was even more incredible than seeing them from the plane.

Our condo is awesome. When Gaga saw it, she said she's happy that it's even nicer than the pictures she saw online. Then she said we should all thank Willy for that. Apparently, he spent days looking for just the right place.

Good job, Willy.

Once we'd unpacked and settled in, Mom, Aunt Lilly, Aunt Lila, and Gaga went to the grocery store to get food and supplies. The dads and kids went to rent boots and skis, which was harder than it sounds. I've never tried on ski boots before. "These are the most uncomfortable things I've ever had on my feet," I said to Fritz, the guy who was helping us with the fitting.

He smiled. "You'll get used to them," he said. "Walk around inside for five to ten minutes. They'll feel awkward at first, but you're good as long as there aren't any uncomfortable pressure points."

"Why does your name tag say 'Bend, Oregon' on it?" June asked Fritz.

Fritz smiled. "That's where I'm from. The people who work here come from all over the world," Fritz explained. "We think it's interesting for our guests to see where we're from."

"I agree," said June, nodding like she approved.

Fritz laughed then got back to boots and skis. He had everyone walk around in ski boots.

"Your boots need to be snug," said Fritz. "Make sure your heel stays in place when you bend your knees and lean forward against your boots."

"Huh?" I was completely confused.

"Your boot connects you to your skis," said Fritz. "If you have too much wiggle room in your boot, your skis won't respond properly to your movements. Does that make sense?" he asked.

"Not really," I said.

Fritz adjusted the settings on my boots and told me I was good to go.

When we got back to the condo, the moms had dinner ready. We ate Caesar salad and spaghetti and meatballs. I don't know if it was the cold mountain air or if I was just hungry from a long day of travel, but everything tasted particularly delicious. After dinner, Gaga asked if anyone wanted to stay up and watch *Frozen* with her.

"We do!" said Charlotte like she was speaking on behalf of her sister and herself.

"That's our favorite movie," said Izzy.

Aunt Lila told them it was too late and that they needed to go to bed so they'd be fresh and ready to ski tomorrow. When Aunt Lila said that, Izzy pointed to Gaga. "She has cancer. Shouldn't she go to bed too?"

"Izzy!" said Aunt Lilly.

But that didn't stop Izzy. She looked at Gaga. "You said you have cancer, but you're not acting like it."

Aunt Lilly looked horrified. I knew she thought the words had come out of her niece's mouth were completely unacceptable, but Gaga laughed. "How do you think someone who has cancer should act?" Gaga asked Izzy.

"I don't know," said Izzy.

"Neither do I," said Gaga. "So I'm just going to keep acting the way I've always acted." She gave Izzy a big hug.

Amanda, Sophie, and I went to the room we're sharing, and Sophie has still been quiet as we've been settling in. But Aunt Lilly just came in and told us it's lights out in five.

Tomorrow we hit the slopes, which I'm sure will be fun. For now, all I can think about is one thing . . .

Sleep!

If I fall I just get back up

and keep going.

—Lindsey Vonn

Sunday, March 22, 7:45 p.m.
DAY 2
At the condo

Having finished my first day on the slopes,
I have a lot to write about! I don't want to
sound like Uncle Drew, but the weather today
was so amazing, it would be a shame not to
describe it in detail. It was cold, crisp, sunny,
and clear. It snowed while we were sleeping,
so when we woke up, the mountains looked
like they were covered with clean, white, fluffy
blankets. That sounds weirdly poetic, but it

was true. Everything around me was just so bright and beautiful.

All in all, it was a fun day, so I don't want to sound like the voice of negativity when I say that showing up at ski school with sixteen other people clad in matching green pants and jackets and neon-orange ski caps was embarrassing. But it was. Actually, we weren't all wearing neon-orange ski caps. Gaga ran out of orange wool by the time she got to hers, so she used whatever "bits and pieces" she had, which meant her multicolored cap distinguished her from the rest of the group.

"We're here," Gaga announced when we arrived.

"We see that," some kid said loud enough for his friends to hear, and they all cracked up. I don't blame them. We looked like we were dressed for a costume party.

Harry, Sophie, and I were all put in the same group with a girl from New Jersey named Mia. Thomas (from Cologne, Germany), who was in charge of the ski school, said the groups were based on age more than skill, but that both were a factor.

When Amanda heard that, she told Thomas that even though we're not chronologically the same age, she, Sophie, and I are inseparable and that she really wanted to be with us. (1) That's a total lie. I would never use the word *inseparable* to describe Sophie's or my relationship with Amanda, and (2) I thought for sure Thomas wouldn't agree to her plan, but he did. He said ski school should be fun for everyone.

Once May heard Amanda was in our group, she wanted to be in it too, since she and Amanda are only one grade apart in school. But then May told Thomas that even though she's younger, she's more skilled than any of us.

"How can you say that?" I asked her. I reminded her that none of us have ever skied, including her, which means it's impossible to know if she's more skilled.

"True," said May. "But as soon as we hit the slopes, I'll be better than any of you. Just watch."

I rolled my eyes. "That's obnoxious," I said. May is a great athlete—we all know that. But I was offended by her pronouncement of greatness. Thomas, however, loved it.

"I always like a kid who is up for a challenge," he said. Then he told her she could not only be in our group, but that he was going to teach us himself. I think some kids in other groups were kind of bummed we got the head guy, but May was ecstatic. She high-fived Thomas and told him she was ready to go.

We said good-bye and good luck to Gaga and Willy. They were taking a group lesson with some other seniors. As we were heading out, I heard Gaga tell their instructor, Skye (from Taos, New Mexico), that she ready to kick some senior butt. Thomas heard it too. I thought it was pretty funny. I'm not sure he thought so. As we were leaving, he told Skye to keep an eye on Gaga.

We got our lift passes and all went outside. Thomas showed us how to put our boots into our bindings and balance on our skis. Then he demonstrated a wedge position, with skis pointed inward, to control the speed. When everyone in our group was comfortable with the feel of being on skis, we went to the top of the bunny hill. But as soon as we got there, I found out our group would be doing more than just skiing. At least, one of the people in our group would be, and that was Mia.

The whole time Thomas was explaining what we'd need to do with our shoulders, poles, and skis and how to maintain our wedge position and shift our weight as we went downhill, Mia was talking to Harry. Thomas even had to ask her to stop talking and listen to what he was saying. But apparently it didn't embarrass her. "I'm a big talker," she said.

"We can see that," said Thomas. I thought it was a semipolite way to tell her to shut up, but she didn't get the message.

"You said ski school should be fun for everyone," Mia reminded Thomas.

"Right," he said. "Just try to listen while I'm talking so you'll know what to do."

"Sure," said Mia. "But just so you know, I can talk and listen simultaneously."

"Cool," said Thomas, but clearly he wasn't impressed.

When it was time for our first run, Thomas told everyone to smile. "I want to see those pearly whites."

"You have great teeth!" Mia said to Harry when he smiled. Then she scooted her skis closer to his and they went down the hill together.

"Was she flirting with my brother?" Amanda asked as she set off down the hill.

When we got to the bottom of the hill, she got her answer.

Mia held up a mittened hand and high-fived Harry. "That was awesome! You're a really good skier," she said.

Harry smiled this goofy grin. I couldn't help but laugh.

"I think Mia likes Harry," I said to Amanda as we settled into a chair on the lift behind Mia and Harry. She made a face like the thought of it made her nauseated. I didn't want to point out the obvious, but Harry seemed to be just as into her as she was into him. They stayed side by side as our group spent the rest of the morning on the bunny hill perfecting our technique.

Mia even sat with us at lunch, which wouldn't have been so bad, except that she kept staring at Harry. At first I thought she was staring at the mustard he had on his lip, but she wasn't. When we were eating the cookies we'd gotten for dessert, she turned to Harry and said, "Your eyes are even nicer than your teeth."

"Eww," said May.

Amanda made a retching sound.

I laughed and so did Sophie. She'd seemed pretty happy when we were skiing, but this was the first time I'd heard her laugh in a while and I was glad to hear it. Mia ignored the comment, the sound effects, and the laughter. She didn't seem embarrassed at all as she asked Harry if his eyes were blue or green.

"Depends on what I'm wearing," Harry told her.

Then they had this long discussion about what color clothing made his eyes look blue and what colors made them green. As they talked, it was like they'd forgotten that Amanda, Sophie, May, and I were even at the table.

After lunch, our group worked with Thomas on making turns.

May picked it up right away. After the first time Thomas demonstrated how to make turns, May took off down the hill, doing it exactly the way he'd shown us.

Harry and Mia weren't far behind. I was kind of surprised Harry was as good as he was. He's usually uninterested in sports, and it was clear he was giving skiing his all.

So was Mia, who told us that in addition to being naturally talkative, she's also naturally athletic. When she said that, I was afraid Harry was going to make a cheesy comment of his own like that she's naturally cute too. Fortunately, he didn't.

Sophie, Amanda, and I all had a harder time mastering turns.

Thomas kept going over the proper technique of how to bend our knees and lean into the turns. I tried bending and leaning like he showed us, but I did a lot more falling than anything else.

"The secret to learning to ski is getting up more times than you fall," said Thomas.

It took a lot of tries for the three of us to get the technique down. By the end of the day, we weren't perfect, but we'd definitely improved.

May, on the other hand, was great. When we were putting our boots away, Thomas told her she's a born skier.

"See, I told you I'd be good," May said to me.

"That's just it," I said. "If you're good at something, you don't need to tell people." I thought I was giving her an important life lesson, but May was more interested in following Mia and Harry into the lodge for hot chocolate.

When we were all seated in comfy chairs around the fireplace, Amanda, Sophie, and I overheard Mia tell Harry that he's an awesome skier. "That's the seventh time today she's used the word *awesome* in conjunction with Harry," Amanda said to Sophie and me.

"It's more like ten," said Sophie. I cracked up. I don't know how many times Mia said it, I was just happy Sophie was joking around and acting more like her old self. When we got back to the condo at the end of the day, I went outside with my phone and took a bunch of pictures of the mountains. Then I went in and showered and put on my comfy sweats. We all hung out in the condo while Dad made chili for dinner.

It was a fun day skiing, and it left me unusually happy. I didn't even get upset when May went on and on about how Thomas said she did amazing for her first time on the slopes, clearly showing she hadn't heard a word I'd said about humility.

During dinner, everyone was laughing and joking, and it was easy to see that I wasn't the only one in a happy mood. My Uncle Dusty even made a comment about all the happy faces.

"Must be because of my chili," said Dad.

"It's because everyone's feet are out of their ski boots and in slippers," said Gaga.

"I think the fresh mountain air is good for everyone," Aunt Lila added.

"Why don't we all go around the room and say what our happy thing is?" suggested Aunt Lilly.

"Mom!" Harry and Amanda said at the same time. It was clear they didn't want to play Aunt Lilly's game. But all the grown-ups liked her idea.

As everyone started to say what their happy thing was, I waited for my turn.

All the answers were kind of repetitive. Everyone liked the same things—the cold mountain air, beautiful scenery, the feeling of skiing down the mountain, getting hot chocolate, and eating chili.

When Aunt Lilly got to me, I decided to step outside the box. "I liked seeing everyone in a good mood," I said. I looked at Sophie as I said it. She's my friend, and today was the first time I'd seen her look happy in a long time.

Whatever was bothering her doesn't seem like it's an issue anymore.

We spent a lot of time with Thomas today working on turns. My happy thing is that it seems like Sophie's mood has made a turn for the better.

Choose people who will lift you up.

—*Michelle Obama*

Monday, March 23, 8:03 a.m.
DAY 3
At the condo

You don't have to be Nancy Drew to know that something bad went down in Emma's room this morning. After breakfast, Sophie went in there, and she was smiling. But when she came out, her smile was replaced with a frown. When I asked if everything was OK, she actually grunted at me. I know she wasn't pretending to be a bear.

"Do you want to talk?" I asked.

"Do I look like I want to talk?" To be perfectly honest, she didn't. And to be even more honest, after that, I didn't really want to talk to her. I went into Mom's room and shut the door. I sat down on her bed while she was getting dressed.

She eyed me. "What's up?" she asked.

I'd talked to Mom about Sophie before we came on the trip, but things have gotten worse, not better. I told her how Sophie has been acting so weird and secretive. "I've asked her if something's wrong, but she won't tell me what it is," I said. Mom sat down on the bed beside me as she pulled on her ski socks, but she didn't say anything.

"Do you think you should talk to Emma?" I asked.

Mom finished putting on her socks and looked at me. "I think Sophie and Emma just need a little time and space."

"If you think that, you must know what's going on," I said.

Mom didn't deny that she did. She looked

at me. "Sophie has some news, but it's hers to tell when she's ready."

"Sure," I said, pretending I understood. But part of me doesn't. If I was going through something, I'd feel better knowing that my friend cared enough to find out what's bothering me. It seems like Sophie doesn't even like that I'm asking. Bottom line: If Sophie doesn't want to tell me what's going on, I'm not going to keep asking.

8:59 a.m.
At ski school

Conditions are deteriorating, and I'm not talking about the weather. Everyone in my group is either in a funk or too happy for my liking. I know that sounds absurd, but it's true.

Sophie hasn't said a word since we left the condo. Amanda is mad because May, who is a year younger than she is, got moved up a group. I was pretty surprised myself when we got to ski school and Thomas said May was going to be in a more advanced group that he was taking. Then he told us that

Sophie, Amanda, Harry, Mia, and I would be in a group with Carmen (from Palo Alto, California), who seems really nice. I can't say I was thrilled to be spending another day of our vacation with Mia.

She, on the other hand, seemed elated.

"YAY! We're in the same group!" Mia said to Harry.

"Are you a cheerleader?" Amanda asked.

Mia ignored Amanda's comment, and so did Harry. He seemed just as happy to be with Mia as she was with him.

I looked at Sophie, who was all quiet and back in her own little world. I wished I could take some of Mia's and Harry's enthusiasm and sprinkle it over Sophie.

Carmen just said it's time to hit the slopes. Wish me luck.

Something tells me I'm going to need it.

1:29 p.m.
Finishing lunch

In lots of ways, the day thus far has been a wipeout. I learned that word from Carmen when I fell on one of the green runs, and my skis and poles were scattered all over the place. She helped me retrieve my equipment and showed me what I needed to do to correct my form. But a wipeout on the slopes isn't the only kind I'm talking about.

Sophie was grumpy and quiet all morning. She hardly spoke to anyone in our group, and it was almost like she didn't care if her skiing improved. Carmen kept trying to show her what to do, but she never took her advice.

Finally, Carmen said to Sophie, "You know, whatever happened before you came on the mountain, it's best to leave it off the mountain."

"Huh?" Sophie asked, but then she shrugged and skied away. I wasn't sure if she didn't understand what Carmen had meant or if she hadn't even been paying attention.

And it didn't help me that Harry and Mia were acting like they were in a group by themselves. They were laughing and talking together like it was just the two of them and no one else was around.

I wasn't the only one bothered by it. "Hey,

Harry, we're supposed to be on a *family* vacation," Amanda said to her brother. But he didn't pick up on the fact (or didn't care) that she wanted him to stop hanging out with Mia and start hanging with us.

The problem with Mia was that she never stopped talking. She spent the whole morning telling Harry about the kids who go to her school in New Jersey. They pretty much sound like the kids in Faraway. As far as I can tell, the main difference seems to be that kids from Faraway have a southern accent, at least according to Mia, who actually tried talking with one. I can say with complete authority that the only thing worse than Mia talking is Mia talking like a southerner.

But that didn't seem to bother Harry either. Everything she said made him laugh, which really pissed off Amanda. "How do you think it makes me feel that my boyfriend just broke up with me, and now Harry found true love?" she asked me when we sat down to lunch.

"I wouldn't exactly classify what Harry and Mia have as true love," I told her.

Regardless, Amanda is still in a bad mood. Sophie still isn't talking. Harry and Mia haven't stopped. We just finished lunch, and now we're going back for an afternoon of more skiing. I don't want to sound like a broken record, but wish me luck.

I'm *definitely* going to need it.

4:35 p.m.
Après ski

That's a French term Carmen taught us, and it means after skiing.

When we finished skiing for the day, our group split up. Amanda went shopping with Aunt Lilly, who promised her she could buy a new ski sweater. Harry and Mia got hot chocolate and went to sit by the fireplace with it. That left just Sophie and me.

"Want to go look in the gift shop?" I asked.

"Sure," said Sophie.

I was surprised when she said yes, and we stood side by side sniffing hand-cut soaps. I hadn't planned to ask her anything, but when she picked up a purple bar of soap, inhaled, and got teary-eyed, I just decided to be direct. "Sophie, I know something's bothering you," I said.

Sophie shook her head. "I just like the scent of lavender, that's all."

I knew that wasn't what was making her emotional. "You were in your mom's room for a long time this morning. There's been tension between the two of you for a while. I'm your best friend. I know something's up. What is it?"

Sophie was quiet. I could tell she was thinking about her answer. "Stuff," she finally said.

It wasn't an answer, so I waited for more. But she just picked up a bar of soap and sniffed it. "Vanilla," she said and handed it to me to smell.

I inhaled the scent. "Nice." I put the soap down and looked at Sophie like I was still waiting for her to answer my question.

"April, I am . . ." But before she could say what she was, Aunt Lila came into the gift shop with Charlotte and Izzy.

"April!" yelled Izzy.

"Sophie!" screamed Charlotte.

Both girls sprinted across the gift shop and flew into our arms like they hadn't seen us for a long time. Charlotte bumped into the table with the soaps. It almost fell over, but I caught it in time.

Aunt Lila laughed. "Girls, be careful or you'll knock down April and Sophie and that nice display too." I looked from Charlotte and Izzy to Sophie. I knew by her expression that the moment had passed. She wasn't going to confide in me. At least not right then.

We all looked around the gift shop together. As we got on the bus to go back to our condo, I made a mental note to try to find the right time to talk to Sophie. Then I scratched it out. Maybe I shouldn't try to talk to her again. Maybe Mom was right, and Sophie will tell me what's bothering her when she's ready.

I thought of the fortune I'd gotten at the Chinese restaurant. *There's much rain before a rainbow.* What if Gaga's sickness isn't the only rain in my forecast? What if whatever is happening to Sophie is another dark cloud on my horizon? Then an unnerving thought popped into my head. What if I'm stuck in a torrential downpour, and there are even more bad things to come?

Dear God, please let this rainstorm be a short one.

6:22 p.m.
At the condo

When everyone got back to the condo after skiing, Gaga said she had an announcement to make. Mom and Aunt Lilly exchanged a look.

"Don't worry," said Gaga. "This one is good." She paused while she waited until she had everyone's attention, and then continued. "I'm proud to report that both Willy and I mastered the bunny hill today."

"That's impressive for two octogenarians," said June.

"Nice vocabulary," Gaga said to June.

Aunt Lilly was clearly not as impressed. "Gaga and Willy are barely in their eighties," she said.

I don't know if she was trying to make Gaga and Willy feel better by reminding them that they're only in their low eighties or if she was trying to send a subtle message to Gaga that she's not old enough to forgo treatment for her cancer.

Either way, I think her comment was wasted on Gaga, who continued talking. "I also want to let you know that Willy and I accomplished what we set out to do, and we're done skiing."

"But the trip is only half over," said May. "If you're not going to ski, what are you going to do all week?"

Everyone looked at Willy and Gaga like they wanted to know too. Gaga smiled. "We're planning to spend a lot of time in the hot tub." She winked at Willy. I couldn't tell if they were kidding or not.

"That's gross," Harry whispered to Sophie and me. I kind of agreed. But Aunt Lilly heard what Harry said and pulled all three of us aside. "I don't want you to say anything negative to Gaga," she said.

"I didn't say it to Gaga. I said it to April and Sophie," Harry told his mother.

Aunt Lilly looked at us like we were all in trouble. "We came on this trip to be supportive.

If Gaga wants to spend her time in the hot tub, that's OK. I expect you to be positive and upbeat around her."

"Don't you think you're getting a little carried away with all this positive, upbeat stuff?" asked Harry.

Aunt Lilly didn't answer his question. "Can you do that?" she asked us.

"Sure," said Harry.

"OK," said Sophie, then she walked off like her participation in the discussion was over and she was excused. She went into our bedroom and shut the door.

Aunt Lilly ignored her exit and looked at me. "April?"

"No problem," I said. I glanced at the door Sophie had just shut. Being positive and upbeat around Gaga is easy. Other people can be more challenging.

9:32 p.m.
In bed

When we got in bed, Amanda asked Sophie and me if we wanted to rank the ski instructors.

"Rank them for what?" I asked. "Who's the best at teaching skiing?"

Amanda laughed. "No, silly. Rank them in order of who's cutest."

"Sure," I said. I thought it was kind of a dumb game, but I could tell Amanda really wanted to do it.

"Are you in?" Amanda asked Sophie. When Sophie didn't look up from her phone, Amanda threw a balled-up pair of ski socks at her. "Stop texting Billy and play the game with us."

Sophie looked up. "OK," she said, even though I could tell she had no idea what she'd just agreed to do.

"Me first," said Amanda. "Wyatt is definitely the cutest instructor." He taught June's group, and June told me at lunch that some of the girls in her group said he looks like a male model.

I had to agree with Amanda.

"You can't pick the same instructor I pick," Amanda said.

I didn't object to the fact that she was making up rules as we went along. "I think Van is super cute."

When Amanda agreed that he's cute, I told her she can't pick the same instructor I picked. She said she wasn't picking, just agreeing. We both looked at Sophie for her turn. She was busy texting again.

"Sophie," said Amanda.

"I have to go talk to my mom. Sorry," she said. But as she left the room, she didn't seem sorry at all.

"What's her problem?" asked Amanda when she left.

Good question.

Nothing so needs reforming

as other people's habits.

—*Mark Twain*

Tuesday, March 24, 1:25 p.m.
DAY 4
From bad to worse

As I ate my oatmeal this morning, I only had two goals.

One: to pick all the raisins out of my oatmeal. I don't know why Aunt Lila put them there to begin with. Shouldn't raisins fall in the category of things that a cook should put on the side, like brown sugar, so people can put whatever they want in their oatmeal?

Two: to make it down an easy blue run.

When we left ski school yesterday, Carmen said she was confident my body would get the hang of it today. But so far, her confidence was misplaced. I worked hard on it this morning. But I think the problem was more in my head than my body.

It started when we got to the lodge. I was putting on my boots when Sophie got her boots out of the locker next to mine, and instead of sitting down next to me, she went around the corner to another bench to put hers on. She might as well have been wearing a T-shirt that read *I don't want to be anywhere near you.* The message was so clear.

Even though I'd vowed to let things go, I had to find out why Sophie was making such a statement. I put my snow boots in my locker and then confronted Sophie. "Did I do something to offend you?" I asked.

Sophie was adjusting the buckle on one of her boots. She stopped and looked up. "God, no."

"I wish you'd just tell me what's going on with you," I said.

Sophie bent down and started fiddling with her other boot like it needed adjusting. "I can't tell you. At least not yet."

I waited until she finished. "Why?" I asked. It seemed like a pretty benign question. Sophie stood and picked up her snow boots.

"I'm going to put these in my locker," she said.

I followed her. "Can you at least answer my question?" I asked.

"This isn't a game, like ranking the instructors." She looked annoyed.

I felt the same way. "How would I know what it is? You haven't told me a thing."

"Drop it!" she practically spat the words at me. Then she exhaled, louder than was necessary. "Let's just ski."

So we did. Sophie, Harry, Mia, Amanda, and I spent the morning with Carmen again. I tried to focus on skiing, but I kept thinking about my conversation with Sophie.

What's going on that she can't tell me . . . yet?

That's what I was thinking about when I

almost ran into a tree. "April!" I heard Carmen yell my name, and I stopped just in time. "Keep your thoughts on the slopes!" Carmen said when she caught up to me.

"Are you a ski instructor or a mind reader?" I asked.

"Both," she said. Then she smiled. "I've been doing this for a long time, and I've found that when you let yourself think about what's going on *off* the hill, you don't do as well *on* the hill. Just focus," she said.

"I'll try," I promised.

At the bottom of the run, Amanda told Carmen she was quitting because she had period cramps. Mia and Harry skied off together to try the run again. That just left Sophie and me. As we rode up in the chairlift, I thought about saying something about what happened, but she was so quiet, I didn't feel like I could.

When we broke for lunch, I decided I had to clear the air. If she wasn't going to tell me her secret, I at least wanted to be able to focus on my skiing.

"I'm sorry about this morning," I said.

"Me too," said Sophie.

While it's not the resolution I wanted, a truce is at least an improvement.

5:45 p.m.
Back at the condo

BREAKING NEWS: I got down a blue run! All afternoon, that's what we skied with Carmen, and by the end of the afternoon, I did it. It was an easy blue run, and I can't say that I looked good doing it. But it was great to accomplish my goal, and Carmen was so proud of me.

"You did it. You did it. You did it, did it, did it!" Carmen chanted the words like a cheerleader. To their credit, Mia and Harry were just as happy for me.

I have to admit, I was happy too.

I wasn't nearly as good as Harry or Mia, who both mastered blue runs and skied down a bunch of them all afternoon. But I got it done. Amanda and Sophie hadn't even tried.

As we left ski school, I was pretty pumped about how much I'd advanced since we started.

So when we all got back to the condo, I announced my accomplishment to everyone in my family.

"April, that's great," said Dad.

Gaga clapped like she was proud too.

"I went down a black run," announced May. As everyone congratulated her, May said that Thomas told her she's one of the best beginner skiers he has ever taught.

The happiness drained right out of me. I was happy for May, but I didn't like her sense of competitiveness.

I don't think Gaga liked it either. She didn't directly acknowledge May's accomplishment, and she even changed the subject.

"I'm proud of all of you," said Gaga. "And so is Willy." Then she brought out a shopping bag. She made a joke about how she and Willy had forgone their time in the hot tub to go shopping instead. "We have gifts," she said.

She reached into the shopping bag and bought out stretchy bracelets for everyone. The bracelets had different sayings on them that related to skiing. As they gave everyone their bracelets, Gaga wanted us to go around the room and read what each of ours said.

Mine said, *Fall down seven times. Get up eight.* It was very descriptive of my day, except that I fell down a whole lot more than seven times.

There were lots of cool sayings, but June's was the most compelling, at least in Aunt Lilly's opinion. "My bracelet says, *Believe you can, and you're halfway there*," said June when Gaga got to her.

"I love that!" said Aunt Lilly. "It's such a positive way to think. A person should always have faith and believe that they can conquer anything." Then she repeated the word *anything* like she wanted to make sure it was heard. It had been. By everyone in the room. But clearly, the person she was talking to was Gaga.

Even though Aunt Lilly hadn't used the word *cancer*, it was obvious that's what she was talking about. An uncomfortable silence settled over the room. Mom and Aunt Lila exchanged a look like this line of conversation might not have a pleasant outcome.

But Gaga laughed. "We came on this trip to ski, not to talk about cancer. We don't have time to talk about it now anyway, because Willy and I have another surprise."

Charlotte clapped. "What's the surprise?"

"We love surprises!" said Izzy.

Aunt Lilly's shoulders slumped. I could tell she thought she'd found a perfect entry into a difficult conversation.

Gaga wrapped one arm around Charlotte and the other around Izzy. "We're going out for dinner tonight," she said. "Who's up for pizza?"

Charlotte and Izzy cheered. Everyone looked happy.

"Pizza sounds good," said Uncle Dusty. Dad and Uncle Drew gave him a thumbs-up in agreement. So did I.

When is pizza ever not good?

9:15 p.m.
Back from dinner

The answer to my last question is: tonight.

Correction: the pizza was delicious. But everything else pretty much sucked.

The problems started when we got to the restaurant. Izzy and Charlotte complained that we were waiting too long for a table. May wouldn't stop saying that she's worked up a huge appetite with all the advanced skiing she'd done and that she was STARVING! June kept reading the menu items out loud and said she wanted to see if she could memorize the whole thing before we were seated. No one was doing anything terrible, but collectively, they were all getting on my nerves.

We finally sat down at two tables, because we couldn't get a table big enough for seventeen people, and Dad ordered pizzas for both tables. The pizzas he ordered sounded delicious, and when they arrived, I thought the worst was behind us. But it was just the beginning.

"Look who's here!" I heard from behind me, but I didn't have to turn around to know who said it.

"Mia!" said Harry.

"What a coincidence!" said Mia.

But I had a feeling it wasn't all that

coincidental. From the minute Gaga said we were going for pizza, Harry had been on his phone. I had a strong feeling he'd texted Mia and told her where we were eating, and then she got her parents to come here too.

"We're about to order," Mia said, like she couldn't stay. She looked right at Harry, even though there were lots of other people at the table. "Want to come to my hotel after dinner and hang out? There's a game room."

"Sure," said Harry, like the game room was the big selling point.

But I didn't think it was and neither did Amanda. "Aren't you a little old for a game room?" she asked Harry.

"It's a game room for teens, not kids," said Mia.

Amanda smiled at her. "Great, I'm a teen, and so are April and Sophie."

"I'm almost a teen," said May.

"We could all come," said Amanda.

Mia raised a brow at Harry.

"I'll see you later," he said, like he'd make sure no one else attended.

"This is supposed to be a family vacation!" Amanda said.

When he didn't respond, Amanda went on and on about how rude it was that Mia and Harry were trying to exclude the rest of us. Harry ignored her and ate in silence, but all of Amanda's complaining was getting on my nerves. When we were done, Harry told Aunt Lilly he wanted to hang out with Mia, and Aunt Lilly said she was fine with it as long as he was back by ten.

Amanda complained all the way back to our condo that it wasn't fair that Harry got to go out, and we didn't. When we got home, Uncle Dusty got out Scrabble. "Who's in?" he asked.

"I don't want to play," said Amanda.

"You love Scrabble," said Uncle Dusty.

"Count me out," said Amanda. She picked up a magazine and plopped down on the couch.

"I don't want to play either," said Sophie. And she didn't even say why. She just went to her room and closed the door.

That just left me with a bunch of old people and some really young ones. I sat down to play Scrabble, but while I set up my tiles, I was thinking about what Amanda said to Harry: *"This is supposed to be a family vacation."*

I don't want to name names, but some people are acting very un-family-vacation-like.

Happy families are all alike;

every unhappy family is unhappy

in its own way.

—*Leo Tolstoy*, Anna Karenina

Wednesday, March 25, 5:53 p.m.
DAY 5
WORST DAY EVER !!!

I'm writing from the comfort of my bed . . . except I'm anything but comfortable.

When June read my horoscope that this was a bad week for me to travel, I should have gotten on a plane and gone straight home. It would have prevented today's horrible events.

When we sat down for breakfast, everyone was talking about what they were going to do during the day. Gaga and Willy were staying in to read. Mom, Aunt Lilly, Aunt Lila, and Emma were all going to go to town to shop, and Amanda wanted to go with them. The dads were going to ski easy runs with Charlotte, Amanda, and June.

That just left Harry, Sophie, May, and me.

"You're all welcome to come with us," said Uncle Drew.

Harry said he wanted to ski some of the harder runs. I knew what he really wanted to do was ski with Mia without all the dads and little kids around. But at least he asked Sophie, May, and me if we wanted to come.

"I'm in," said May.

Harry looked at me. I didn't want to be stuck with the dads and younger kids either. "Me too," I said.

We all looked at Sophie. "I don't want to ski today," she said.

Emma put her coffee cup down. "Honey, we only have two days left here. You should enjoy the slopes," she said.

I think Emma meant it as a suggestion, but

Sophie pushed her bowl of oatmeal away and stood up from the table. "I'm fourteen. You can't tell me what to do."

The table got quiet fast. Emma cleared her throat. "Sophie, I'm your mother."

Sophie snorted, then ran into our room. Emma followed her in. When she came back, she said that she and Sophie were going to spend the day together.

I didn't know what they were planning to do, but those of us who were going skiing left for the slopes. This morning was fine. Fun, actually. Harry, May, Mia, and I all skied together. We did some green runs and lots of easy blue runs. The problems started after lunch. "Let's do some more challenging runs," said Harry.

"I'm in," said May.

"Yeah, me too," said Mia.

They all looked at me. "I don't know," I said. The runs we did this morning were the same as the ones we did yesterday with Carmen. I wasn't sure I was ready for anything harder.

"We won't do anything too hard," said

Harry. I finally agreed, so we took the lift to the top of a blue run and skied down. It didn't seem that much harder than some of the runs we'd done in the morning. When we all got to the bottom, we got back on the chairlift. I thought we were going to do the same run again, but when we got off the lift, Mia said she thought we should try something even more challenging. She skied to the top of an advanced blue run. Harry and May followed her.

I didn't want to ski down the mountain by myself, so I went too. But when we got to the top of the run, I didn't like what I saw. "It's too steep, and there are tons of moguls," I said.

For once, Mia was quiet.

"I wouldn't say there are *tons* of moguls," said Harry.

The way he said the word *tons* made it sound like I was exaggerating the difficulty of the run.

I planted my poles in the ground and crossed my arms across my chest. "Maybe there aren't tons. But there are a lot of bumps, and I don't feel comfortable going down it."

Harry looked down at the run and then looked at me and shrugged. "There are a few bumps. You can handle them. We'll go slow and stick together," Harry said.

May nodded like it would be a team effort.

They all stood there looking at me like I was the one acting like a chicken and holding them up from having fun. I didn't feel like I had a choice.

"OK," I said.

But as soon as we set out down the run, nothing we did even remotely resembled a team effort. May took off down the mountain, which left me to follow Harry and Mia. There were bumps and slick patches everywhere. I couldn't imagine how I was going to get down the rest of the run.

"Stop!" I yelled to Harry and Mia.

They both turned around. "Relax," said Harry. "You can't stop and start. You need to just go."

I started to feel panicky. "I can't do this," I said.

"Yes, you can," said Harry. "Carmen taught us how to do this."

"She taught us on easier blue runs," I said. "This is way too hard."

"It's not that much harder than what we did with her. You know what to do," said Harry. "On the count of three, we're all just going to go."

Harry counted, and then he and Mia started skiing down. As I watched them maneuver around the bumps, I felt sick. I was too far down the run to climb back up. I knew I had to go if I wanted to get down, but nothing in me wanted to go.

I counted to three in my own head, and I went.

But as I skied down, I started to go faster than I wanted. I tried to slow down, but I couldn't.

As I picked up speed, I felt the wind rushing against me and bits of icy snow flying up and sticking to my goggles. I remember thinking that the exposed parts of my face were too cold and then thinking that I shouldn't be thinking about my face.

The next thing I remember is trying not to fall. I leaned up the mountain and tried slowing myself down with my own body weight, but I couldn't.

Then I fell. I don't even know how far. As I tumbled down the mountain, I think I tried to stop myself with my arms and legs. I lost my skis. I dropped my poles. My body hurt as it rolled through the snow.

When I finally stopped, I was disoriented.

I called for Harry and Mia. But no one answered. I didn't see them anywhere. My eyes started to tear up inside my goggles.

I thought about my equipment. I had to find my skis and poles. I looked around and tried to stand up, but I couldn't move my leg. I was in a lot of pain.

What happened after that was a blur.

Some other skiers stopped when they realized I needed help. I don't remember much other than one of the skiers telling me they were placing their skis vertically in the snow behind me so other skiers wouldn't run into me and so ski patrol would have an easier time finding me. All I remember about the other skier was that he had on red boots. I kept staring at them and trying not to cry while I waited for ski patrol to arrive.

When they finally did, they asked me a bunch of questions. What hurt? Did I hit my head? Did I feel numbness anywhere?

Then they put me in a toboggan that was attached to a snowmobile.

I remember thinking that it looked like a big metal dish. They strapped me in, covered me with a blanket, and drove me down the mountain.

Emily and Benito on ski patrol called Mom and Dad, but when they couldn't get them right away, they drove me to a nearby clinic. They waited with me until Mom, Dad, and June arrived. The clinic x-rayed my leg. The doctors determined that I had a broken tibia and that my leg needed a cast.

It was all so surreal.

Now I'm in my bed at the condo, and random bits and pieces of this awful afternoon are starting to come back to me.

I remember June holding my hand while I was waiting to be x-rayed. I remember crying when I found out my leg was broken and that I'd need a cast. I remember Dad trying to say funny things to cheer me up. I remember not being in the mood to laugh.

But mostly what I remember about today is that I didn't want to go down that run.

I'm mad at Harry for making me doing something I didn't want to do. I don't even think he would have cared whether we did it if Mia hadn't been there. He was showing off for her.

And I'm mad at May. When I said I was scared, she could have volunteered to go down an easier run with me. But she didn't do that. She just skied off and left me. She's my sister. I've been there for her so many times, and she wasn't there for me today. All she cared about was what she wanted to do.

And for that matter, I'm mad at Sophie too. She wasn't directly or even indirectly responsible for me breaking my leg, but I'm mad at her for the way she's been acting for most of the trip. True friends are supposed to share what's going on in their lives with each other. I've tried to find out what's going on with her, but she won't tell me a thing.

We came on this trip to have fun as a family.

Maybe some people have had fun. But I'm not one of them.

7:07 p.m.
Visiting Hours are OVER!

When Mom, Dad, and June brought me home from the clinic earlier, my whole family was already at the condo.

"My poor baby," said Gaga. I let her give me a hug, but when everyone started to ask me about what happened, I told them I wasn't in the mood to talk.

All I wanted to do was lie down. Mom helped me get in bed and propped my leg up on a stack of pillows to prevent swelling.

I wish I could report that I'm off to a good start of what will be at least four weeks of recuperation, but so far I've had a whole string of visitors who won't leave me alone to rest and start recovering!

Visitor #1

Harry was the first person to come in. "Can I talk to you?" he asked.

"No," I said.

"It's not like you're going anywhere." He said it like it was supposed to be funny, but I didn't laugh. "Sorry you got hurt," he added.

I closed my eyes. "I'm trying to sleep."

"Are you mad at me?" he asked.

I crossed my arms across my chest and frowned. "Do I look mad?"

"You don't look happy."

I gave Harry the biggest fake smile I could muster.

"I'm sorry I made you go down a run that was too hard," he said. He waited for me to respond, but I didn't.

"You want some apple juice or something?" I knew it was a peace offering. His way of saying he was sorry. But I declined the offer.

I think it's pretty easy to understand why I wasn't in a forgiving mood.

Visitor #2

May was the next person who came to come see me. When she walked into the room and sat down on the bed, I winced. Just the slightest movement made me uncomfortable. "Does it hurt?" she asked.

"Yeah," I said. May sat there looking at me like she was waiting for me to give her some details, but I didn't.

She finally spoke. "I'm sorry."

"For what?" I asked.

"I'm sorry I've been such a bragger. I know I've been talking a lot about what a good skier I am."

I shook my head at her like she didn't get it.

But May kept talking. "What I'm really sorry about is that I skied off and left you." She started to tear up. She seemed honestly sorry.

Even though I was casted up and not in the mood to play the big-sister role, there was something I had to say. "May, you get really upset if someone isn't sensitive to your feelings." I reminded her how she felt when she was bullied by the girls on her soccer team. "Maybe you should try to be more sensitive to how other people are feeling."

"I will," said May.

I closed my eyes and put my head back on the pillow. I wasn't sure if she would or not. And right then, I really didn't care.

Visitors #3, 4, 5, and 6

When May left, Sophie came in. "I'm tired," I said when she pulled up the desk chair next to my bed and sat down.

"There's something I need to tell you," she said. "You're not going to like hearing it, especially not right now. But I want you to understand why I've been in a funk."

I pointed to my leg. "Cast trumps funk."

"I know," said Sophie. "But I still have to tell you." She paused like she was waiting for my permission to proceed. When I finally nodded, she said, "My parents are getting divorced."

This wasn't a complete surprise. The reason

she and her mom moved to Faraway at the start of the school year was because her parents were separated.

Sophie kept talking. "The reason I've been in a bad mood lately is that my parents have been trying to decide what to do with me." She paused. "Sometimes it's like I'm a piece of chicken, and they aren't sure if they want to bake me, broil me, or stir-fry me with vegetables."

Sophie started to tear up. It was clear this was painful for her. I listened quietly as she kept talking. "My dad wanted me to come live in Paris with him, but my mom said no. Mom wants to stay in Faraway with me, but my dad wouldn't agree to it. He said that he doesn't think it's good for me, especially given what's going on with Gaga."

I sat up as well as I could. I had a bad feeling I wasn't going to like what was coming.

Sophie paused, and then continued. "So after much debate, which is what has been going on all week, my parents have decided that the best thing for me is to live in New

York. My dad is moving back to New York and so are Mom and I, and they're going to share custody of me."

I said a silent prayer that I'd misunderstood what she'd said. "Does that mean you're leaving Faraway?"

Sophie nodded. "Mom and I are moving back to New York at the end of the school year."

"Is that what you want?" I asked.

"Part of me wants to stay in Faraway, especially for my grandpa. He's going to be so lonely when . . ." Sophie hesitated. "My grandpa is going to be so lonely if something happens to Gaga. But I want to be with my dad too." As she looked at me, her shoulders slumped. It was clear she saw this as an imperfect solution. "It's a compromise," she said softly. "But it's what's best."

I felt tears welling up in my eyes.

"I'm sorry I've been so weird and secretive lately," said Sophie. "At first, Mom and Dad were talking about everything without me. They weren't including me in the conversation, and it made me mad that they were acting like my opinion didn't matter."

I guess that explains why Sophie and Emma weren't getting along.

Sophie looked down, avoiding eye contact. "I haven't told you because I didn't want to ruin the trip."

The tears I'd been holding back fell freely down my cheeks. Sophie got up and got me a tissue. I thought about the saying on the bracelet that Gaga and Willy had given me. *Fall seven times. Get up eight.* I know I'll get over my broken leg, but Sophie leaving will be a much harder recovery.

"I can't imagine Faraway without you." My voice was barely a whisper.

"It's a bummer for me too." Sophie reached over and squeezed my hand. We sat like that until we heard a knock on the door. Mom came in carrying a tray. Aunt Lilly and Gaga were with her.

"We brought you some soup," said Mom. She placed the tray in front of me.

I looked down at the bowl of steaming broth and noodles. "I don't want any soup," I said.

Aunt Lilly frowned at me. "Eat the soup. You'll feel better."

I know she wanted me to eat the soup and put on a happy face for Gaga, but I'd had all I could take. When I found out Gaga was sick, I thought I'd hit a patch of rainy weather. Now my leg is broken, and Sophie is moving. Bad things just keep happening. Clearly, there's no rainbow in sight for me.

I pushed the tray away, and the glass of water on it fell over.

"April!" said Aunt Lilly.

"What? You want me to be happy and positive? Sorry, I'm not, and soup won't help."

I waited for Aunt Lilly to admonish me, but before she had a chance to say a word, Gaga jumped in. "For heaven's sakes, April doesn't have to be in a good mood." She removed the tray from my lap and handed it to Aunt Lilly. The she pointed to the door. "You can all go," she said to Sophie, Mom, and Aunt Lilly like they were dismissed.

When it was just the two of us, Gaga bent down and kissed me on the forehead. "I'm going to give you a few minutes, and then I'd like to come back and talk. OK?"

I nodded. I have no idea what Gaga is going to say, but I don't see how anything she says will make me feel better.

You can't pick out the pieces you like and leave the rest. Being part of the whole thing, that's the blessing.

—*Tuck*, Tuck Everlasting

STILL NIGHT 5

I thought I knew everything there was to know about my family. Clearly not.

When Gaga came back into my room, she sat down in the chair that Sophie had sat in earlier. "I know you're upset about everything that's happened—my sickness, Sophie leaving." She patted my cast. "And to top things off, a broken leg."

"I'm not happy," I said.

Gaga nodded like she appreciated the truth. "I have a story to tell you. I've thought about sharing it with you for a while. Now is the right time."

I inhaled, then let out a breath and put my head back on the pillow. I couldn't imagine what Gaga was going to tell me, but I had a feeling I'd be listening for a long time.

"April, I want you to know what happened to your mother and aunts when they were little." Gaga paused. "One day, your grandfather left town and never came back. He left me with no career, no money, and three young girls to look after."

Gaga sat up straight in her chair. "I went to work and I did what I had to do to raise your mom, Lilly, and Lila."

I couldn't believe what I was hearing. "I always assumed Grandpa died when Mom and her sisters were little. How come no one ever told me the truth?"

"We weren't keeping it from anyone," said Gaga. "It's just not something we talk about. Lilly was five when he left, so she has a few memories of him, but even those have dimmed over the years. Your mother was three, and your aunt Lila was one, so all they've ever known was me."

I was speechless. I tried picturing Gaga as a young mother raising three girls and trying to take care of everything. She's the strongest person I know, but still. "That must have been really hard," I said.

"It was," said Gaga. "For a long time after your grandfather left, I was overwhelmed and very angry. I didn't think I could do it. Every day of those first few years was a struggle."

"How'd you do it?" I asked.

"Not very well. I don't much like thinking about that time. I yelled a lot, and my girls felt it. I don't remember exactly how or when, but I remember waking up one day and realizing that being angry was an awful feeling, but that dwelling on the things that make you angry can have far more disastrous consequences. I knew I had to let go of my anger, or it would hurt my girls even more than their father's leaving."

She paused. "I made a conscious effort to be positive and productive. I chose to see the good and not complain."

"It's one thing to say it, but it must have been hard to do."

Gaga sighed. "I don't mean to make it sound like I snapped my fingers and it happened. It was very hard to think positively, but I did my best. Eventually, it got easier. I'd be lying if I didn't tell you I had my bad days too. We didn't have a lot, but I wanted to raise my girls to be positive and appreciative of what they had. I'd like to believe it made a difference. Your mom and her sisters are all pretty positive."

"Especially Aunt Lilly," I said.

"Especially Aunt Lilly," Gaga said with a smile. "But the truth is that all three girls grew up happy and didn't dwell on what they didn't have."

Hearing this story gave me a newfound respect for Gaga. Doing what she had to do and letting go of her anger had to be so hard. "You're so strong," I said.

Gaga reached over and took my hand. "So are you, April." She paused, and then looked me square in the eye like it was so important that I heard what she said next. "The reason I told you this story tonight is because it won't do you any good to be mad that I'm sick or that Sophie is leaving or even that you took a tumble on the slopes." She paused. "Anger is a wasted emotion."

Gaga continued talking. "The reason I was able to move on with my life when your grandfather left was because I chose to forgive him. I knew it was a smarter choice than staying angry."

Anger as a choice? I hadn't thought about it like that. As Gaga continued talking, I thought about what it meant for me—letting go of my anger toward Harry or May or Sophie, or whoever or whatever it was that allowed me to fall and Gaga to get sick.

And the truth was that while I had things to be angry about, I knew there were worse things. Like what happened to Gaga. She might see anger as a wasted emotion, but I think it's relative. Maybe she had more to be angry about, but the bottom line is that it doesn't really matter. What Gaga was saying was right. What good would it do to stay angry?

Gaga squeezed my hand. "Are you OK?"

I nodded. She'd given me a lot to take in, but I still had a few questions for her.

"Did you and Willy know before we came on the trip that Emma and Sophie would be leaving Faraway?"

Gaga laughed when I asked that. "Of course we knew. Parents, especially old ones like us, are pretty perceptive when it comes to their kids," she said. "But it wasn't our news to share. Sophie needed to tell you in her own time and in her own way."

I wrinkled my nose as I thought back to the other day when I'd tried to talk to Mom about this when she was getting dressed. I realized she'd known then, but now I understood why she couldn't tell me.

Gaga looked down at me over the rim of her glasses. "When Emma was growing up, she was a lot like Sophie. Pretty. Headstrong. A bit rebellious too." Gaga paused.

"What does this have to do with anything?" I asked.

"I'm getting to that," said Gaga. She

looked at me and then continued her story. "When she was in college, she went to study in Paris. While she was there, she met a man and fell in love."

"Sophie's dad?" I asked.

Gaga nodded. "She stayed after college. Willy was very upset. Emma is his only daughter. Eventually, she got married and had Sophie."

Gaga's story was starting to make sense. "So you're saying that Sophie and Emma leaving Faraway is hard for Willy too. Is it like losing Emma twice?"

Gaga shook her head. "It will be hard for Willy when they go. But that's not what I'm saying."

"I'm confused," I said.

"Part of loving someone is letting them go. Whether it's a child or a friend." Gaga paused. "Or even a grandmother."

"Gaga, please don't say that," I said.

Gaga didn't flinch. "It's the reality of life," she said. "It's sad. And it's hard, but sometimes, you don't have a choice." Gaga stopped talking and looked at me. "You know, Sophie has had a lot to process too," she said.

Gaga was right. This can't be easy for her or for her grandpa. "What's Willy going to do?" I asked.

Gaga smiled. "He has plans too."

"To move to New York with Sophie and Emma?"

Gaga laughed. "Heavens no. Faraway has been his home all his life. He was thinking more along the lines of buying a fishing boat."

The image of Willy in his boat made me smile. I hugged Gaga. "Thanks for telling me all this," I said.

Gaga didn't respond, she just kept hugging me and rubbing my back. It made me equal parts happy and sad—happy she was there to talk to and sad knowing that wouldn't always be the case.

STILL NIGHT 5
BUT MUCH LATER!

Before Gaga left my room, a thought occurred to me. "I think Sophie would benefit from hearing your story," I said.

"You're free to share it with her," said Gaga. "It's way past my bedtime."

Gaga left and sent Sophie in, and I told her the story.

"Was the point of that to tell me that I shouldn't be mad because my parents can't get along? I've lived in three different cities for the past three years and come this summer, I'm going back to city number two," Sophie said when I was done.

She had a point. Paris to New York to Faraway and back to New York was a lot of moving around in a very short time. "You're one of the most upbeat, positive people I know," I said. "I just don't want to see you lose that."

"April, my parents are getting divorced. It's just kind of a hard time." Even though I was the one in a cast, it was clear she was hurting too.

"This must be hard," I said. Sophie nodded. Then she got in bed next to me, and we stayed side by side for a long time, neither of us saying anything. I don't remember when, but at some point we both fell asleep, and we didn't wake up until Amanda came in the room.

She poked us both awake. "You each have a bed, you know."

I saw her point. Two teen girls, one large cast and a stack of pillows in a twin bed. The image of it made me laugh. When I started laughing, Sophie did too. As Amanda stood there starting at us like we were crazy, we laughed even harder. I don't know why. There wasn't really anything to be laughing about.

But it felt good.

Things are never as bad as they seem.

—*Miss Maudie*, To Kill a Mockingbird

Thursday, March 26, 9:32 a.m.
Last Day in Utah

We just had a group breakfast at the condo. Mine was served with a side dish of "I'm sorry," which I have to say goes pretty well with French toast and fruit.

When I sat down, May brought me a plate. "I'm really sorry about yesterday," she said when she set it down in front of me. "I'll make it up to you."

"How?" I asked. "By bringing me breakfast?"

"Lunch and dinner too. For as long as you need me to." May grinned.

131

"Deal," I said. I couldn't help but laugh. "I guess it's pretty obvious I could use your help."

"Yeah," said May. I could tell she'd heard what I said yesterday and was trying to be more thoughtful.

After breakfast, Mom set me up on the back porch. It was cold, but it felt good to be outside. Harry came out and joined me, and he was apologetic too. "I didn't mean for you to get hurt on the run yesterday," he said. "Are we over what happened?" he asked.

"By *we* do you mean *me*?"

Harry nodded, and his face turned red. He was either hot or embarrassed, and since it was thirty degrees outside, I knew it wasn't the former.

I could have gone back over what happened, but I didn't. "We're cool," I said. He hadn't done anything to intentionally hurt me. It was an accident.

And what would have been the point? My leg would still be broken.

Sophie came outside and told me she was sorry too. I have to admit that it was an apology I hadn't expected. "What are you sorry about?" I asked.

"I know I've been completely into my own deal lately. Sorry if I shut you out."

"I get it," I told her. When we talked last night, I could see how upset she's been about what's happening to her family.

"I had a long talk with my mom this morning," Sophie said. "I told her I'm not happy about leaving Faraway, but I'm trying to be optimistic about going back to New York. We promised we'd try to stay open and honest with each other through the divorce. I'm relieved we're at least talking like we used to."

I'm happy for her. It seems like the talk we had after I talked to Gaga helped her to put things into perspective.

I couldn't believe how much things could change in a day. Yesterday I felt horrible, physically and mentally. I can't say that I feel great today. My foot is even more swollen than it was last night, and my leg hurts, but I feel better on the inside. I'm not angry at anyone—not at May or Harry or Sophie. And to be perfectly honest, I'm proud of myself for making it down an advanced blue run, even if I broke a leg doing it.

Plus, there's a perk to having a broken leg—I was relieved from dishwashing duty. I'm sitting here with my leg propped up, writing in my journal, while the other kids are inside, clearing plates and washing dishes.

It could be worse.

7:54 p.m.
$4.25 richer than I was this morning
In a show of solidarity, my whole family sat the day out. It was Harry's idea.

He said that since it's the last day of our trip, he thought it would be nice if we all hung out together, so we stayed in and played poker. That was Willy's idea. He told us that back in the day he was a pretty good player and could teach us all a thing or two about the game.

He wasn't kidding.

First, he gave us a lesson on how the game

works. "In poker, all hands contain five cards, and the highest hand wins. Cards are ranked from high to low. Aces, kings, queens, and jacks are high, and it goes down all the way to the low end of the deck—fours, threes, and twos," said Willy. "Spades, hearts, diamonds, and clubs all have the same rank, and we'll be using jokers as wild cards."

"Tell them about the different kinds of hands," said Gaga.

Willy smiled at Gaga. "I'm getting to that," he said patiently. Then he told us about lots of different kinds of hands—five of a kind, straight flush, full house, and a bunch of others. At first, it sounded pretty confusing.

"I don't want to play this game," said Charlotte.

"Can we play Candy Land instead?" asked Izzy.

"It sounds harder than it is," Willy told them. Then he promised that everyone would catch on quickly. I wasn't so sure, but Willy made Charlotte partners with Aunt Lila and paired Izzy with Uncle Drew. And Willy was right—once we started, everyone got the hang of it. Then Willy divided us up into groups of five and explained that we'd be playing five-card draw.

"More instructions!" said Izzy.

Charlotte moaned like she was being tortured.

Willy laughed and asked Charlotte and Izzy if they'd like to be his assistants. They were very happy to stand by his side while he explained the rules of five-card draw. Then Willy got a bag of almonds and said we'd be using them as poker chips.

"Do we get to eat them?" asked Izzy.

"Nope," said Willy. "You get to pass them out." Charlotte and Izzy gave everyone ten almonds, and Willy explained that each almond would be worth twenty-five cents.

"Do we have to pay for our almonds?" asked June.

"Good question," said Willy. "Normally, card players have to put up their own money. But since you're all special players, at least to Gaga and me, we're putting up all the money."

Willy grinned. "And the good news is that you keep whatever you win."

Willy appointed a dealer in each group who dealt everyone five cards. After we got our cards, we placed bets by putting however many almonds we wanted to in the middle of the table. "At the end of the hand, whoever has the highest hand that hasn't folded wins," said Willy.

Then he explained how betting works. Wrapping my head around calls, raises, and folding was even more confusing than learning how to play the card game, but eventually I caught on, and so did everyone else, and we spent most of the day playing poker for almonds.

Sophie came in first place. She won fifty almonds. When she counted up her almonds and announced she'd won $12.50, Willy gave her a big hug. "You're a chip off the old block," he said.

Uncle Dusty came in second place, followed by June, then Emma, and then me.

I was pretty happy with the $4.25 I won.

"It was a mercy win," said Harry who finished with twenty-five cents and second to last, only ahead of Gaga.

"The cards don't know I broke my leg," I said.

"But the dealer did," said Harry. He made a few comments about the fact that my dad was the one giving out the cards in our group, but Dad denied any wrongdoing.

I didn't mind Harry's teasing. It was a great afternoon. Some people were good at poker, although most weren't, and some stank. But everyone had fun, even Gaga, who ended up with nothing.

She was a great sport. When she finished playing, she said, "Loser makes dinner." Then she pointed to Harry and said, "Next-worst player is *sous chef*."

So Harry and Gaga spent the rest of the afternoon making lasagna. He seemed uncharacteristically happy as he and Gaga chopped, boiled, sautéed, and baked. And it made me happy seeing how much Gaga loved spending the day with her family.

Even though learning to ski was on her bucket list, I think playing poker and cooking with the people she loves meant even more to her.

"Mom, this is delicious," said Aunt Lilly when we all sat down to eat. For once, I had to agree with her positive statement. Uncle Drew gave Gaga a big thumbs-up, and Uncle Dusty seconded his opinion with his own thumb.

"I couldn't have made it better myself," said Dad.

When Charlotte finished her portion, she went to where Gaga was sitting and gave her a big hug. "I liked my dinner," she said.

"Gaga is a great cook," Izzy announced to the group like it was a fact.

I got a little emotional when she said it, because it reminded me that soon we might have to say things like that in the past tense.

Gaga was *a great cook.*

I hate that thought. But hating it doesn't change things. I thought about what Gaga and I had talked about. I get that it's important not to dwell on what makes you angry.

But I already know that days like this without Gaga won't be an easy thing to accept.

Well, it's no secret that the best thing about a secret is secretly telling someone your secret.

—*SpongeBob*

Friday, March 27, 9:45 p.m.
HOME!!!
In my bed
Curled up next to my dog

I can truly say that I've never been so happy to be home. Hands down, the best part about getting home—besides having the long day of travel behind me—is that Gilligan hasn't left my side. I think he saw my cast and crutches and just had a dog's sense that something was wrong.

The trip home today was a big challenge.

141

It wasn't too hard navigating through the airports on crutches—that part was pretty easy because the airline carted me around in a wheelchair. But there were other things that made it challenging.

Like going to the bathroom on a plane. I had to walk down the aisle with my crutches. Mom escorted me because she didn't want me to fall. At fourteen, it's pretty embarrassing to be taken to the bathroom by your mother. It's even worse when it happens on a plane. As we walked down the aisle, several people wanted to know what happened. "She had a little tumble skiing, but she'll be fine," Mom said, like I'd asked her to be my spokesperson.

"Mom, I can explain what happened," I mumbled.

"You just focus on getting to the bathroom safely," she said.

I was relieved when I finally got inside the bathroom and out of Mom's watchful eye. But when I sat on the toilet, my crutches, which I had propped up against the wall, fell over, and one of them hit me on the head. Now, I have a bruise on my forehead to go with the cast on my foot. Not a great look.

But it wasn't just the cast and crutches that made the trip home challenging. Sophie literally talked the whole way back about how and when she was going to tell Billy she's moving back to New York. She made me promise I wouldn't tell him. "Why would I tell him?" I asked.

"Because you've been best friends with him for a long time," she said.

I wasn't sure if it was the altitude or the fact that she'd drunk a whole can of apple juice and eaten three bags of mini pretzels, but she wasn't making a lot of sense. "Why would I want to be the one to tell Billy something he won't want to hear?"

It was Sophie's secret to tell. I didn't mind her talking to me about how she was going to share it. But soon other people would know, and that made it seem that much more real.

As our plane was landing in Mobile, I closed my eyes and thought about the trip. There were some bumps (and not just the ones on the slopes), but all things considered, it was a great trip with my family, and I'm so glad Gaga planned it.

It's something I'll never forget.

Skiing in the mountains was probably the complete opposite of snorkeling in the Florida Keys, which was what I did on our family vacation two summers ago, but I loved this just as much. I remember going underwater and thinking that everything was so peaceful and quiet. The mountains were majestic and open, and it made me feel like I was on top of the world. I wouldn't be able to choose which I liked more.

I think the bottom line is that I like experiencing new things. But as great as it was to go away, I'm glad to be back. I don't want to sound too much like *The Wizard of Oz*, but I think Dorothy said it best.

There's no place like home.

Saturday, March 28, 4:45 p.m.
Talked to Leo

Leo called today to see how I was doing. It was really sweet. "How's your tibia?" he asked.

It made me laugh. No one but him would refer to the actual bone I broke.

"Hard to tell," I said.

"How's the rest of you?" He didn't have to explain what he meant.

When I called from Park City to tell him about my fall on the slopes, I'd also told him that Sophie is moving. "I still can't believe she's going," I said.

"Remember when we talked about patterns?" asked Leo. I couldn't imagine where he was going with this. "I still don't see one," he said. "Gaga's cancer. Sophie moving. A broken leg. They're all unrelated incidents."

"I'm not so sure." I told him about the fortune I got in the cookie at Happy China and about my horoscope June read in the Atlanta airport on the way to Salt Lake City. "They were both accurate," I said.

Leo laughed. "I'm a science guy. I definitely don't believe any of those things happened as a result of a fortune you got or a horoscope you read."

"Then how do you explain all of those bad

things happening at once?" I asked.

"The answer to that is simple," said Leo. "People get sick. They break bones. Families move. It happens all the time."

I wasn't sure it was as simple as Leo thought it was. But I did have another question for him, and I didn't think he'd have a quick answer for it.

"What explanation do you have that will make me feel better about the fact that I will be turning fifteen in less than a month with a cast on my leg?"

I was sure I had Leo on this one. But in typical fashion, he had a response. "April, I think you'll look cute in a cast and a birthday hat."

I love that Leo always knows what to say to make me feel better. Kind of like Gaga.

Thinking about it made me laugh. Who knew the boy I like would turn out to have something in common with my grandmother?

Sunday, March 29, 3:45 p.m.
Trying to read

I was sitting at the kitchen table, quietly reading *Us Weekly* when Mom sat down with me. "We need to talk about school tomorrow and how you're going to get around."

I looked up from my magazine. "That's the last thing I want to talk about." Or think about. Going back to school with my leg in a cast sounds awful. "I want to enjoy the last day of spring break thinking about the Kardashians, not about the week ahead," I told Mom.

Shockingly, she let me do it.

9:02 p.m.
In my room

May and June just came into my room to tell me good-night. "We promise we'll help you with anything you need while your leg is in a cast," said May.

"Yeah," said June. "Your wish will be our command." She put her hands together, genie-style.

I laughed. "You don't have to do that," I said. But I appreciated the offer. And what made me feel even better was that I had a strong feeling it had all been May's idea. Ever since we got home, she's made a big effort to be sweet and thoughtful. It's clear she's thought about what I said in Park City.

As my sisters hugged me good-night, I thanked them for their offer of help.

Come tomorrow, something tells me I'm going to need all the help I can get.

Monday, March 30, 5:54 p.m.
Home from school
Thankfully

There are pros (at least one) and cons (many) to going to high school on crutches.

Pro: You get a lot of attention and offers of help. I couldn't believe how nice people were at school today. Maybe it's because I live in Alabama and it's just southern hospitality at its finest, but so many people at school were so nice. Kids I barely know offered to carry my backpack between classes. At lunch, Harry and Sophie brought me food. Two football players even offered to carry me, and not just my backpack, across campus. Since I'm not a football, I respectfully declined the offer. But I have to admit I considered it. It was hard work getting around Faraway High on crutches.

Now the cons: Sore underarms, an itchy, swollen foot, and the obvious unattractiveness of being in a cast weren't even close to the biggest downside. The worst part for me about having a broken tibia is that it means I'm out of dance for the rest of the season!

That's worse than bad, because the remainder of the season is the most important part. We have the district and regional competition coming up, and then the state competition if we make it, which we always do.

Surprisingly, Ms. Baumann was sympathetic when she heard what happened. I thought she was going to give me a lecture about how I should have been more careful. But she didn't. She just said accidents happen and gave me the rest of the season off from dancing, but she also made me her assistant. That means I'm supposed to help her organize music, schedules, and costumes.

My official duties started today, and since Ms. Baumann is incredibly organized, there was no additional organization for me to do, which means I sat in a chair during practice and did my homework while the rest of the team danced.

At break, the girls on the team all signed my cast and everyone was sympathetic when I told them the doctor in Park City said I'd be in a cast for at least four weeks.

"I can't believe we've lost one of our best dancers right when we need you most!" said Emily. I wasn't sure it was true, but it was nice to hear it. Everyone was so sweet . . . except for Brynn. I should have expected it. She didn't sign my cast. She didn't say anything to me. Not even an, *"I'm sorry you fell and broke a bone."*

Honestly, I think that hurt more than the pain in my tibia.

Wednesday, April 1, 7:05 p.m.
The secret is out

I wondered how Billy was going to take it when Sophie told him she's moving back to New York, but I don't have to wonder anymore. Sophie just came over to tell me how it went when she told him this afternoon after school.

In typical, thoughtful Billy fashion, his first concern was for Sophie and how she's doing. "He was so sweet," said Sophie. "He kept saying he hopes I get that this is about the fact that both my parents love me and just want what's best for me."

"Did he say he was sad?" I asked.

Sophie laughed. "Actually, he said he was happy."

"Huh?" I hadn't expected that reaction.

"He said he was glad he figured out why I was in such a funk before the trip because he was starting to feel self-conscious that it was something he'd done."

I could relate to that. Still, I knew Billy was kidding when he said he was happy. "You have to love Billy's sarcasm," I said.

"I do," said Sophie. "There are lots of things about Billy I love," she said. She told me she's really going to miss him when she leaves but that she's glad she told him she's moving. "I feel better now that my secret is out," she said.

I smiled at her. "You know how the saying goes. The truth shall set you free."

"Yeah," said Sophie. I know she feels better. But I can't say that I do. Now that she's told Billy, I know word will spread fast.

Billy was right. Sophie's parents only want what's best for her, and that means living in New York City where they can both be part of her life. That's definitely what's best for her.

I just wish it also felt like what's best for me.

The true courage is in facing danger when you are afraid.

—The Wizard of Oz

Sunday, April 5, 7:45 p.m.
In Dad's office at the diner

There's something comforting about sitting at Dad's desk. I don't know what it is, but I've always liked it. Maybe it's being surrounded by his papers, all the framed photos he has of May, June, and me, or the large bowl of Tootsie Rolls that he keeps on his desk. Right now I think I like it because there's an extra chair next to his desk that I have my cast propped on. Whatever it is, it feels good to be sitting here writing, even though what I'm writing about is kind of serious.

Reality is setting in. I can feel it.

Tonight, my whole family came to the diner for dinner. Dad made fried chicken and mashed potatoes. It's the meal Dad always makes when we come home from summer camp, and it's one of my favorites.

As I sat and ate, I kept wondering how many more dinners we'll have like this while Sophie is still in Faraway and Gaga is alive.

But I realized it wouldn't do any good to dwell on it. It's kind of what Gaga was talking about when she told me what happened to her. Being mad is one thing. Staying stuck in it is another. For now, Sophie and Gaga are both here, and I still have time to enjoy being with them.

As I was thinking about it, Gaga sat down in the chair beside me and gave me a slice of pecan pie Dad had made for dessert. "Everything OK?" she asked.

"Peachy," I told her.

Gaga laughed. "I didn't know kids still used that word."

"Most don't," I told Gaga.

"Do I detect a note of sarcasm?" she asked.

Now it was my turn to laugh. "Why would I be sarcastic?"

Gaga took a sip of coffee. "I can think of a couple of reasons." She pointed her fork at Sophie who was sitting across the table from me. "Your best friend is leaving town, and your favorite grandmother doesn't have much time on the clock."

Gaga's honesty was darkly humorous. "Gaga, you're my only grandmother," I reminded her. Then I frowned. "And what you said isn't funny."

Gaga got a serious look on her face. "No," she said. "It's not funny—it's life." She took a bite of pie and then pushed her plate back. "Have you ever heard the expression *carpe diem*? It's Latin for 'seize the day.'"

"Gaga, I'm not in the mood to hear a lecture."

But Gaga was in the mood to give one. "April, every day is an opportunity," she said. "If you don't make the most of each and every one, good things will pass you by. Happiness. Love. Success. There's always possibility."

I finished the last bite of pie on my plate and licked my fork clean. "Did you hear that on one of those sappy movies on TV, or did Aunt Lilly say it?"

I hadn't meant to be funny, but Gaga laughed. "It happens to be true. If you don't like how I said it, I'd like to hear you do a better job."

I knew it was a challenge, and I rose to it. Plus, I kind of had something to say on the topic.

"OK," I said. "How about this?" I cleared my throat like I was an important speaker. "I'm not happy Sophie is leaving Faraway. I'm also not happy that you're sick. I hate thinking about the fact that the day will come when you won't be here. But I know it's important to stay in the moment. Sophie isn't leaving until the end of the school year, and you're still . . ."

I paused. I wasn't sure what word to use.

"Alive?" Gaga said like she was filling in the blank.

"Yeah," I said. That was the word. It was just hard for me to verbalize it. "What I mean is that I want to enjoy all the time I have left with both of you." I pointed to my leg. "Cast or no cast, that's exactly what I'm planning to do."

When I finished my soliloquy, I felt oddly self-conscious. I shrugged. "I don't know if I did a good job saying what I meant."

To my surprise, Sophie clapped and Gaga put her fingers in her mouth and whistled. "I couldn't have said it better myself." Then she grinned and wrapped an arm around me. "April, have you considered a career as a professional speaker?"

It made me laugh. "Right now, I'm focused on finishing ninth grade." I winked at her. "I want to make the most of each and every day. Remember?"

Gaga smiled. Then she surprised me.

She reached into her purse and pulled out the ski cap she'd made for herself and put it on my head. "I want you to have this," she said. "Think of it as an early birthday present."

Even though I love presents, this one made me emotional. "Gaga, are you giving me the cap because you know you think you don't need it anymore?"

Gaga laughed. "God, no!" she said. "That's not it at all. I just don't like what it does to my hair. I have no idea why you kids wear these things for fun." She reached over and put the cap on my head.

"That looks good on you," said Sophie. She reached across the table, rolled up the edge of Gaga's cap, and then pulled one side down so it rested on an angle.

"There," she said like she'd arranged it perfectly on my face. "You look very stylish, and it takes the emphasis off your leg."

Gaga pulled a powder compact out of her purse and opened it so I could see myself in the little mirror. This might sound corny, but as I looked at Gaga's multicolored ski cap on my head, I couldn't help but think that it was a hand-knit version of the rainbow I'd been waiting for.

I pulled it down over my ears and laughed—a deep, full laugh, and it was the first time I'd laughed like that in a while. It felt good. I thought about Leo's comment that I'll look cute in a cast and a birthday hat. Maybe just for my birthday, I'll trade in my ski cap for a birthday hat. Maybe I won't. I'll see how I feel that day.

But for now, I'm just taking things one day at a time.

Is there any silver lining when you're born into what is clearly the wrong family? **April Sinclair sure hopes so!**

Ten Reasons My Life Is Mostly Miserable

1. My mom: Flora.

2. My dad: Rex.

3. My little sister: May.

4. My baby sister: June.

5. My dog: Gilligan.

6. My town: Faraway, Alabama.

7. My nose: too big.

8. My butt: too small.

9. My boobs: uneven.

10. My mouth. Especially when it is talking to cute boys.

THE MOSTLY MISERABLE LIFE OF APRIL SINCLAIR

Can You Say Catastrophe?

LAURIE FRIEDMAN

Too Good to Be True

LAURIE FRIEDMAN

Truth and Kisses

LET'S KISS
FRIENDS NEVER
TOO SOON
MAYBE NOT

LAURIE FRIEDMAN

Not What I Expected

LAURIE FRIEDMAN

Too Much Drama

py New Yo

LAURIE FRIEDMAN

Love or Something Like It

LAURIE FRIEDMAN

A Twist of Fate

LAURIE FRIEDMAN

About the Author

LAURIE FRIEDMAN grew up in the Deep South, and, like April Sinclair, was awestruck the first time she saw snow-covered mountains. But that's not the only thing she and April have in common. She too had a hard time learning to ski, and though she finally figured out how to get down the mountain without too many falls, she decided she prefers spending her time in a warmer climate. Ms. Friedman lives with her family in sunny Miami, just minutes away from the beach. She is the author of the Mostly Miserable Life of April Sinclair series as well as the popular Mallory series and many picture books.